Valentine Night Ghosts

Dean Fraser

ISBN: 9798266317659

Contents

Dedicated to the memories of
Douglas Adams
Terrance Dicks
And Leslie Charteris
Authors collectively inspiring the eleven-year-old me to
want to write stories when I grew-up. Writing this novel
suggests I'm a grown-up. When did this happen?!

ANDIE VALENTINE

Some mysteries defy logic

All is as it needs to be then

PART ONE

1

On one particular Tuesday morning in late July, Andie Valentine found herself sitting on the wide inner sill of her bedroom window absently gazing down on the River Dee in home city of Chester with very little to do and very much bored. Nothing of importance required attention. No paranormal cases to occupy her, for the first time in four years she'd decided to take a home vacation break from filming videos for her channel, Valentine's Night Ghosts. Her fridge and cupboards were all fully stocked, and the wine rack contained eight bottles of her favourite Saint-Émilion Claret.

She watched hundreds of tourists wandering along the riverside in the morning sun; the heatwave meant the hotels and guesthouses were doing good business. For one brief moment she even toyed with the idea of going outside to join them and take a walk herself. She might do, maybe in an hour or two, if she could summon up enough enthusiasm to venture outside and mingle with crowds in the blazing sun.

*****

Since making her debut video for her Valentine's Night Ghosts channel, Andie had become famously renowned as a goth. Complete with de-rigour black clothes, smoky eyes, darker shades of lipstick, deathly-pallor foundation, bare nails as she doesn't enjoy the feeling of nail polish, and signature waist-length brunette hair. It's frequently speculated on her channel Andie's hair is all courtesy of extensions, plus her natural hair is surely ginger and gets dyed brunette, together with her eyebrows and eyelashes. Andie's followers have yet to know she exists, however, Teri Valentine, Andie's her younger sister, is both ginger and curly. We'll never know for sure if Andie is brunette, she resolutely refuses to answer any personal questions on her channel. Andie's mobile hairdresser cousin Cerise takes care of her tresses for her; she wouldn't be spilling any family secrets!

Alongside being renowned as a goth, Andie is universally hailed by followers of her channel for being a sublimely beautiful young woman.

A sublimely beautiful young woman beyond bored with the many subscribers to her channel rarely commenting specifically on cases, other than positively critiquing her gothiness, yet endlessly eulogising about her pulchritude. Andie never deigns to reply to comments relating to her appearance, however within three hours of posting a new video, she always answers any questions asked about her latest case featured.

Privately Andie confided in Teri, who'd noticed her older sister's latest marriage proposal from a subscriber, she'd rather get told she's beautiful, than being informed by her followers she's fricking gross!

She recorded her first paranormal video four years ago. Andie was a fully committed goth and simply filmed the case video how she dressed on that day. She was about to discover her viewers found her supernaturally drop-dead gorgeous!

'Ghost Babe' she was nicknamed by her rapidly growing number of followers. Through Valentine's Night Ghosts, despite never allowing adverts or accepting sponsorship for videos, Andie became significantly financially secure.

Since fame came her way, if she'd continued venturing everywhere bedecked in her full gothic glory, she would find no peace for members of the public wanting selfies.

Andie quickly came to understand going undercover as 'any-girl'; avoiding at any costs black clothing, changing her make-up, and her distinctive hair tied into a tight bun and hidden away under a beanie or hoodie; she could do grocery shopping, travel untroubled on public transport and stroll around Chester without being recognised. Naturally Andie still attracted plenty of attention, gothic or not the woman is difficult to ignore! At least 'any-girl' distanced her from Valentine's Night Ghosts.

Meanwhile in her home, Andie sighed to herself, stood up and partially closed the window to shut out some of the noise, yet leaving just enough gap to allow the humid air from outside to make the already stiflingly warm room all the more sweltering.

She padded barefoot across the polished oak floor over to the bookcase dominating one wall of the room, picking a book off the shelf at random. Surprisingly petite at five feet two inches, she easily laid herself out comfortably full length on her burgundy leather Chesterfield, opening her book appropriately at page one. She'd likely already read every book in her extensive personal library at least twice, irrespective of this fact, Andie soon found herself deeply absorbed within the pages of her abridged edition of The Golden Bough.

Her laptop resided on the copper topped table off to the right-hand side of the sofa, as per usual it was turned on and as per usual it was largely ignored. This table, her bookshelf and the sofa were the only pieces of furniture in the large room. There would be no point in her owning a television, it would get lonely through lack of attention. On its stand, by the second of the windows overlooking Chester's river, Andie's violin stood on it stand awaiting her next practising jam session.

Andie Valentine's house was her refuge, her safe space. It was a demon, ghost and poltergeist free zone. Given her vocation, she needed this. It perfectly reflected her taste. Walls were painted silver throughout, woodwork stained satin black and black roller blinds hung at the windows. Her home was situated outside of the famous Chester Roman Wall, but not too far, and valuing her privacy, it wasn't overlooked by her nearest neighbours.

After relaxing reading for slightly under an hour, Andie's laptop pinged, announcing that out of the seven billion of us residing on our blue and green sphere in space, Andie Valentine was the chosen one to be communicated with. The woman doesn't really do 'startled' however she was deeply absorbed on her book, it did take her a moment to recognise the pinging noise she'd just heard heralded the arrival of an incoming email.

She raised herself up off the sofa and padded back to the bookshelf for one of her countless bookmarks; slipping one into the book, she carefully replaced it exactly where it came from; and picking up her laptop, she strolled out of the room intending to read the email in her home office. Andie Valentine never worked in the chilling-out area of her home.

Many of us might well refer to this room as the lounge or perhaps sitting room. Andie didn't use either of those labels, hers got called the chilling-out area or her library, as the mood took her.

She opened the door to her office and entered. This room paid homage to Andie's four years' worth of paranormal investigating. Walls more or less covered with matching framed photos featuring the thumbnails she'd used for videos during those years.

Room for a few more photos, however if the woman was planning on taking on the number of cases as the previous year, she'd better begin planning right now on moving home, she'd need a larger office for extra wall space!

Aside from all the case photos, her office was minimalist. The furniture consisted of a vintage polished steel desk, on which resided an original black Bauhaus desk lamp, sat in front an eighties' Josef Gorcica blue leather office chair; a S32 Cantilever Marcel Breuer chair waited against the wall for guests. A panoramic window looked out over the back of the building, at that time of the day, before the sun came round, her office was pleasantly cool.

If anyone cared to glance out of the panoramic window, they would observe a gated landscaped rear yard, this is where Andie Valentine's pride and joy stood awaiting her next adventure. This pride and joy of hers took the form of a 1995 Ford Scorpio Estate. Perhaps not the obvious choice for a young woman, Andie never was too much of a conventional thinker. In metallic black, with roof rails, 'Scorpy' was the closest vehicle resembling a hearse she could find without actually driving a hearse!

Once a month a specialist vehicle detailing and cleaning company took care of it for her in the convenience of her own back yard.

The AND 1E private number plate adorning Scorpy may well have cost Andie half as much as her home, but once she knew it existed the woman simply had to have it for her car!

*****

She placed her laptop on the desk and sat herself down in front of it. Only now she finally opened her email to see who this mystery contact was from.

The concise email read 'Hi Miss Valentine, interested in my wine bar and restaurant for a lockdown?' Owner of Kostović, Bold Street, Liverpool' and that was all!

She received many emails requesting her particular kind of expertise, they would generally tell all in their contact email about what haunting they believed they had, and how they thought she could help them.

Andie fired off a quick reply 'Lockdowns at bars usually involve illicit after-hours drinking. I'm guessing that's not what you're offering me?'

The response to this question came back in under thirty seconds 'We have ghosts for you Miss Valentine, oodles of lovely ghosts!' Once more, it was only signed Owner of Kostović, Bold Street, Liverpool.

Andie was hooked. She emailed 'Okay, I'm intrigued. It is Liverpool in England and not New York State that your bar is located in?' She smiled as she wrote this, she'd just looked up Kostović on google and knew perfectly well where it was located, Andie liked to have her fun.

She didn't need to wait too long for a response, when it arrived thirty seconds later it made her laugh out loud 'Miss Valentine, we each us of knows perfectly well you just looked up Kostović on google! Please may we meet to discuss a lockdown? I know you are based in Chester, the one in England not Massachusetts! Please come visiting me soon in the UK Liverpool'

Andie re-read this reply a few times before responding, concluding whoever she was communicating with likely wasn't native English, they were intelligent and agreeably shared her silly sense of humour.

'Today?' She'd responded to the question of when with one word. 'I am here until six, yes today is most excellent, thank you Miss Valentine. Ask anyone at the bar for the owner' The mystery person stated.

*****

Andie stared at herself in her dressing-room mirror and looked down at the baby blue skater dress she wore. She tutted at the absurdity of being seen in public wearing the thing! 'Any-girl' to Andie never meant dressing down or dowdy, she experienced imposter syndrome every single time she left home wearing regular fashions. Andie got that being dressed identically to millions of women across the globe was necessary if she wanted to live any kind of a normal life, however there wasn't any rule suggesting she should always adore her lifestyle compromise; heart and soul Andie Valentine was a goth!

She headed straight into the shower to freshen herself up. Delighted with the prospect of a possible new paranormal case, her home vacation officially ended right there and then!

Andie dressed in all of her gothic finery for the first time in six long weeks and took her time getting her make-up and hair completed to her satisfaction. Within two hours of opening the enigmatic email from 'Owner of Kostović, Bold Street, Liverpool' Andie Valentine exited the front door resplendent in her midi length black wedding dress teamed up with black platform-heeled ankle boots, her micro-camera was tucked away in her bag and there was a spring in her step during the half hour's walk to Chester Railway Station.

Andie 'Ghost Babe' Valentine was back!

2

Andie found no vacant seats on the packed train from Chester to Liverpool, in holiday season it was generally laden with day-trippers heading either outbound for their music experience in Liverpool or returning from a Roman encounter in Chester; that Tuesday was no exception. The journey takes forty minutes flat, standing up part of the way wasn't a big deal to her and overcrowded as the train undoubtedly was, it was by far a preferable option than attempting to find any parking place in Liverpool in height of holiday season. Big crowds meant Andie wasn't asked for selfies, though she hardly travelled on her way unnoticed. She'd got used to stares years ago and become excellent at not seeing them.

Along with her fellow passengers, she disembarked the train in the depths of Liverpool Lime Street Station. Andie took her time meandering along the platform and making her way up into the city, gladly allowing everyone else to pass out through the hub first, and onto the street. Andie followed in their wake a few moments later. According to the station clock, she observed it was only 1pm, the owner of Kostović stated they would be there until six, so in no hurry, she walked to the waterfront. Crossing the busy road which divides the main city from Royal Albert Dock, managing to avoid getting run over by impatient drivers waiting their one in a thousand chance to park.

Passing the landmark Royal Liver Building, towards her destination, which it turned out was actually a bench!

Ask the casual observer their opinion, they would likely describe an unfeasibly beautiful young woman sitting on a bench, apparently on her way to wed her vampire lover. To avoid ruining it by catching the delicate layers of her black tulle wedding dress on the rough bench, Andie carefully piled it high on her lap. This same casual observer would likely also assume, as she patiently waited for her vampire lover, the strikingly lovely woman was enjoying the view across the River Mersey to Birkenhead. This wasn't the reason Andie was there, this very bench held deep significance from five years earlier in her life.

At eighteen years old Andie Valentine had reached one of those crossroads-in-life moments. Should she accept the amazing offer of her musical mentor Candy to tour with her all-female orchestra right across the Balkans for half a year or go with what she knew was her real calling in life; record videos whilst she investigated haunted locations? Andie has never regretted the decision she made sitting on that very bench a winter's day five years ago.

Touring across the Balkans with Candy and her orchestra was horizon expanding for Andie; she lived in paradise on stage playing literally second fiddle; after six months the tour concluded at a music festival in Belgrade, Serbia. Having thoroughly soaked up every experience touring with this world class jazz band could offer, and with the security of all the fees from the tour resting in her bank account, Andie Valentine followed her true calling as she recorded her first paranormal case video.

Candy toured from time to time, but with nothing like the intensity of that Balkan tour! An official member of her orchestra, billed and introduced as 'Rosa Lee on second violin!' In her 'any-girl' mode, Andie joined Candy for every tour. She'd played violin on Candy's most recent album, also credited as Rosa Lee.

After staying half an hour, she was done with reminiscing and leisurely retraced her steps in roughly the direction of Liverpool Lime Street Station. Andie wasn't leaving town just yet, Kostović was located close by the station on Bold Street.

*****

Walking through the centre of any other city, even if she wasn't recognised from her channel by those demanding selfies, in her full gothic finery she would be subjected to numerous unsolicited opinions about her fashion sense or unwanted wolf whistles and yelling from off of building sites, outside of pubs and occupants of passing white vans, informing her in succinct words she's sexually attractive. She'd concluded back in her teens Liverpool is basically too cool for most of those things to happen. Occasionally yes but very rarely. If anyone recognized Andie Valentine from her channel, they left her in peace. That's Liverpool!

*****

Andie's parents owned Valentine's Bistro in Chester, like Kostović, this was a wine bar and restaurant. She'd even waitressed for them in school holidays to help them out in their busiest period, the extra money came in useful too! Teri Valentine did the exact same thing for a few weeks out of every summer school holiday. At eighteen, college life soon beckoned, that year Teri didn't waitress.

This investigation would be far from her first set in a wine bar or restaurant, and truth be told, Andie never really enjoyed these cases like other locations. It wasn't meeting the ghosts, or even not, if it turned out they were simply the subject of collective autosuggestion and no more real than a politician's election promises. The reason for her distaste at exploring in the deeper recesses of clubs, pubs or wine bars was all about her overwhelming repulsion for the odour of beer borne of years spent in her parent's bistro and an even stronger wish to avoid like the plague alcohol-induced faux group merriment for precisely the same reason!

She entered Bold Street from the city end. Bold Street has quite the back story of its own to tell. Many have reported this time travelling portal existing in this thoroughfare, suddenly finding themselves briefly in Liverpool during 1940's war time or even further back in the Victorian era. Too many credible witnesses claimed to have experienced this during several decades. Andie believed most of their stories were fundamentally true.

Aside from Andie's home city of Chester, Liverpool was her favourite place in England. She adored the live and let live attitude and she'd been visiting regularly since she was thirteen. Andie had a good idea of where Kostović would be, and she was proved correct. The blue painted building sat substantially on the end of the second block, located on the right-hand side, strolling up Bold Street.

Andie took out her micro-camera to record her thoughts, this kind of footage seldom made it to her case videos, it was useful though to help plan the investigation.

She observed the building from across the road before entering. Andie talked into her camera "Three stories. French blue, with cream writing and wooden detailing. The usual smokers stood outside invitingly wide-open doors. I am wandering around to the rear of the building on Wood Street, there's a small staff car park" Turning off her camera, Andie wondered which was the owner's car and guessed the newish Audio Cabrio, later turning out to be incorrect. Steeling herself for the upcoming assault upon her olfactory senses, Andie went around to the front doors on Bold Street, holding her breath whilst passing through the gaggle of smokers, she entered Kostović.

Before making her way to the bar announcing her arrival, Andie glanced around the room she'd just stepped into. Kostović was packed. Several customers blatantly stared. Perhaps they recognised Andie from Valentine's Night Ghosts or were enjoying the arrival of a stunning young woman in a gothic wedding dress and platform boots.

The bar was a substantial room. Stools were traditionally situated across the front of the bar, tables liberally dotted around the large room, and all occupied by people dining. She stood on the polished oak floor not unlike the one in her home. The ceiling higher above her head than she'd anticipated. Whoever furnished Kostović fully met with Andie's approval. No screens to satisfy soccer addicts, the background muzak only noticeable by its absence, and a lack of intrusive video games or fruit machines.

3

She made her way to the bar, finding a gap between the customers, promptly capturing the attention of a member of the bar staff "Hi, I'm Andie Valentine, here to see the owner" She declared. The woman grinned in response to this and glanced at the person sat on the bar stool adjacent to Andie, who naturally also looked in the same direction. The occupant of this stool introduced themselves "Hello Miss Valentine and welcome to Kostović! I am the owner. It is way too cool you agreeing to meet me this promptly" Andie shook the proffered hand, slightly in a daze about precisely who the owner of Kostović turned out to be "Hi, thank you and you're really welcome. Good to meet you!" Andie replied, her eyes wide open in surprise.

Philosophical as ever, she reasoned although the picture she'd got in her head about who the owner of Kostović would be was spectacularly wrong, at least she was right about them not being native English!

The owner introduced themselves "Miss Valentine, my name is Rada Kostović. I am thinking we must adjourn to my office for our conversation in privacy, yes?" Andie nodded her head agreeing. Rada asked "Would you care for coffee a Miss Valentine, or perhaps you would prefer something alcoholic?" Andie replied "Strong white coffee is always welcome!" Rada addressed the member of bar staff Andie just spoke to "Claudia, please bring us two coffees to my office when you have moment" Claudia confirmed she would.

Andie followed Rada behind the bar and through swing doors; after passing through the busy kitchen and empty staff room, they arrived in a short corridor. They didn't communicate while they walked. Andie appreciated this. Like herself, Rada obviously didn't feel the need to fill in moments of natural silence with pointless chit chat.

Andie estimated Rada was at the upper maximum thirty years old and likely less. Feminine and chic in her vibrant floral boho maxi dress; her light ash blonde hair was tied with white ribbons into two neat plaits hanging down the front past her breasts. It was obvious her blondness grew from the roots and not courtesy of any hairdresser. Rada wore make-up enough to bring out her striking pale blue eyes, matte clear lip gloss, and her face free of foundation. Sandals showcased psychedelic patterned nails, matching perfectly manicured fingernails, with no heel the sandals revealed Rada's height at slightly more than Andie in her six-inch high boots, in Rada's case a genuine five foot nine inches. Multiple crystal power-bracelets adorned both her wrists and a statement turquoise necklace sat around her neck. Silver hoop earrings and a moonstone mounted in a silver ring worn on the second finger of her right hand completed her jewellery. Rada's heady fragrance wafted over Andie, attempting to identify her exquisite perfume she couldn't place it.

Having already passed one passcode protected door with 'Staff Only' written on it, at the end of the corridor stood an identical door bearing the same sign. After punching in her passcode, Rada gestured for Andie to enter, closing the door behind them.

*****

Andie possessed powers of observation finely honed through years of paranormal investigations, in moments taking in the details of Rada's office. A window offered an excellent view out onto the staff car park, a laptop sat on the antique bureau desk positioned near the window, the Bauhaus influenced chair placed in front of the desk. A large amethyst cluster on the floor by her desk. The walls painted cream, like the rest of Kostović the floor was polished oak. Positioned on the top of the desk were two photos of a gentleman appearing in his mid-sixties. Taking up the entire length of one wall, situated on the right-hand side as you walked in, an apparently leather Chesterfield, identical to Andie's, aside from the cream colour. Andie pondered what excellent taste this woman had!

Rada gestured in the direction of the sofa; Andie made herself comfortable. Kicking off her sandals, Rada placed herself close by Andie, siting in the lotus position on her sofa, her body attentively angled towards her. Rada's sensual fragrance smelled divine up close.

"I'm a fan of your work Miss Valentine, I've watched all your videos since your very first, coinciding with my UK citizenship in Liverpool. I'm twenty-seven years old, yet even now I am avidly awaiting every new case you post to Valentine's Night Ghosts. I rewatch your first case vid before I emailed you Miss Valentine; you appear terribly young, perhaps not even so long out of the high school?" Rada said and asked. Her softly spoken, gently soothing voice carried strong traces of an accent Andie recognised yet sounded authentically Liverpudlian as well.

Andie laughed "On the day I filmed that video I turned nineteen years old! I went into that investigation with an open mind and much more enthusiasm than experience, I'm twenty-three and know there's so much yet to learn about film-making!" Rada asked "That old abandoned church where you find the ghost during that investigation, it is standing today? Someday I would adore to visit Burton on Trent to see for myself!" Andie Valentine would have invited Rada along to show her around on her first day off from Kostović if it were "I'm sorry to say Rada, it all got demolished one month after my investigation to build a supermarket and car

25

parking" Obviously disappointed, Rada stated "Too uncool Miss Valentine!" Andie nodded her head in agreement.

Looking thoughtful she declared "If I ever wake up one morning not excited about going out on an investigation Rada, I know it's the moment I need to stop" Rada leapt immediately onto her feet in alarm standing directly in front of Andie "Do not stop Miss Valentine! I know I am but one of the five million followers of your Valentine's Night Ghosts; I personally would be devastated if you cease filming new cases! I saw that brief video telling us you'll vacation for a few weeks. I am thrilled to observe you must be taking on cases once more Miss Valentine, otherwise you wouldn't be sitting next to me appearing good enough to eat upon my sofa!" Andie didn't know what to make of Rada "Yeah, my vacation is over Rada" Returning to the sofa, Rada sat herself down again in the lotus position "Oh my gosh! Nothing prepares anyone for meeting you in person. Obviously you are bewitching in your videos, however you are otherworldly beautiful in the flesh Miss Valentine! Alike exquisite gothic doll! Oh no, I hope I do not insult you?!" Andie giggled. Now sure Andie wasn't about to walk out on her, Rada continued "You hair it is perfect, not a strand out of place, and your dress that would look ridiculous on me is yet incredible on you!" Andie replied "Thanks Rada, I know you can't tell, I promise you that under my foundation I'm blushing scarlet right now!" They laughed together.

Andie smiled at Rada Kostović, and this made her smile warmly back at her in response, starting in her eyes and lighting up her entire face, in a moment she transformed from a pretty blonde hippie into a boho living goddess! Andie witnessing this transformation held her breath for a brief moment and as her heart involuntarily skipped a beat stated "I'm delighted you enjoy the channel. I get excited about new cases four years on from that first one, I'm not going to stop making new videos anytime soon!" Andie decided this was the moment to get around to the reason Rada asked her there, she added "You mentioned in your email you have oodles of lovely ghosts Rada?" She said this as a question.

Rada stated "There are plenty of spirits at Kostović; also three ghosts we know of!" She laughed after this; Andie couldn't help laughing along. Rada looked her directly in the eyes and asked in her gently soothing voice "And will Zen Sanders be joining you on this case Miss Valentine, if you accept it?" She hadn't anticipated this question, but then she hadn't anticipated the owner of Kostović would be the lovely fragrant hippie asking it!

*****

Andie Valentine might have been twenty-three, but thus far in her life she'd experienced only two of what might be considered relationships. So ironic that Andie's traffic-stopping beauty made it quite challenging for her to meet possible suitors interested in who she actually is, instead of only lustfully wanting her in bed. Her first relationship happened at eighteen during touring across The Balkan region of Eastern Europe with the orchestra, two weeks in she'd hooked up with the drummer. Their love lasted as long as their tour; abruptly ended by her lover the night before returning to their normal lives. Naturally Andie felt devastated but learned a lot about human nature!

Three days on from turning twenty-two years old, Andie Valentine met Zen Sanders who completely swept her off her feet!

Andie got invited to paranormally investigate the theatre in London famous for performing the same play since the 1970's. Zen was the cast member who volunteered to offer Andie the guided tour around the building upon her arrival.

He was like a matinee idol from a bygone era; tall, sexy and handsome. They found much in common while he showed her around every square centimetre of the entire theatre. Zen Sanders was half French; Andie's mum is also French and head chef in her family's bistro. Thirty-year-old Zen had lived in England since he was three. For over a decade, when not busy acting, he was an urban exploring ghost hunter, his preference being anywhere he might encounter darker spirits or demons!

Zen made quite an impact upon Andie meeting him. He asked Andie for her phone number, delightedly she gave it him and hoped he would get in touch.

When she returned to the theatre after last curtain at ten thirty that night, he'd apparently already left to go home, however, when she'd finished her investigation at two twenty that following morning, there he stood waiting for her in the foyer of the theatre. He took her for a moonlit stroll by the River Thames and early breakfast at a café he knew. Andie was enchanted.

After a much-needed sleep at her hotel, Andie was Zen Sanders's special guest for the matinee performance of his play, in the box positioned right by the stage. In Andie's obviously unbiased opinion, Zen Sanders was incredible at playing Giles Ralston; unnoticed by anyone else in the audience he covertly winked at her exiting the stage near her box after a scene. Andie was utterly enchanted.

Andie soon got another case in London, Zen and her had been messaging and talking every day since meeting. The   case wasn't too far from Zen's theatre and coincidentally, it fell on a Sunday, a day when he wasn't working. They met for lunch and found more commonalities between them. He asked if he could tag along for her investigation, and although up until this moment Andie always worked solo on her cases, Zen was such an experienced ghost hunter and so thoroughly charming, Andie suggested investigating together. He offered to be her camera man, and only if she felt comfortable with this, he would make a few observations of his own as Andie went about her investigation. Handsome Zen looked amazing on-camera, and this case did very much end up being them exploring together. In the wee small hours of the morning they were through, and Andie did not return to her hotel room alone. Andie was blissfully enchanted.

"Show me any straight male who isn't terribly turned-on by a beautiful gothic girl! Alan, you've met Miss Andie Valentine, did there ever exist a more stunning specimen of gothic girliness than she?" This observation was made by Zen in conversation with the director of his play in the afternoon when Andie headed back home up to Chester. "Ahh but Zen, the question of course becomes, are you serious about this beauty or is she merely yet another in your long line of conquests?" Zen sat looking thoughtful "I shock myself Alan to confess I am deadly serious about beauteous Miss Andie Valentine! She's got a magic about her Alan, I swear I shall remain devoutly faithful to her!" Alan laughed cynically "Really Zen?" Zen didn't find this in the slightest amusing "Yes Alan, this is for real! I shall treat everyone in the cast to dinner if I am unfaithful to positively ravishing Miss Andie

Valentine!" His leading lady overheard Zen's promise and declared "Curry thank you Zen! When you discard Vampira, I shall immediately step in to console her and offer her my sisterly shoulder to cry on; and naturally Vampira may share my bed with me for however long it apparently takes to get over a man such as you Zen Sanders" By now the entire cast had assembled for rehearsals and roared in laughter. Alan said "Dahling, kind of you to allow her to share your bed" She replied "I merely offer sisterly company to adorable Vampira; never was there any suggestion this might be about me wanting gothie hottie screaming at me for more as I'm having my wicked way with her night after blissful night!" Everyone roared in laughter.

During her long drive home, Andie pondered the events of the previous night and unfortunately was deeply in the process of falling in love with a rakishly handsome serial seducer.

Andie and Zen began their long-distance relationship, she started taking on cases fitting around his acting schedule, located in London. They became investigation partners; making cutting-edge case videos alongside one another. Intentionally the two of them kept it strictly professional on-camera. If they were colleagues or lovers the subject of endless speculation by the millions of subscribers to her Valentine's Night Ghosts. Andie of course, never denied nor admitted this.

31

Andie always appeared stunning on-camera, alongside her handsome partner-in-film; she'd amassed countless new followers to Valentine's Night Ghosts. Yet Zen's dark personal energy, but far more than this, too many of his actions during their investigations unsettled Andie. He couldn't resist provoking demonic spirits!

Two months before she'd found herself sitting on Rada Kostović's sofa, Andie tired of needing to compromise for their relationship. His endless excuses for never travelling to Chester to stay at her house or investigate cases not on his own doorstep had worn too thin for Andie to tolerate. His natural charm and good looks meant he typically got his own way; this time Zen Sanders experienced the novelty of getting dumped rather than his philandering finishing off his relationships; in her case he'd been astoundingly faithful! Andie Valentine was no longer able to put up with her one-sided compromises for the sake of a relationship and she informed Zen she was through with him directly to his face. They hadn't communicated since. She felt sure he would be living his life as large as ever in London; this city still had locations she would yet adore to investigate. Andie held no plans to go visiting England's capital for the foreseeable future.

She'd taken her home vacation time-out to allow herself to get into the right headspace to continue on and make compelling solo case films for her channel after working with a co-investigator for ten months.

*****

Andie considered the most honest way to answer Rada's question and opted "Mr Sanders and I worked together for a while; we'll never collaborate on another case again" Rada Kostović quietly absorbed the information, made no comment and didn't appear too devastated to hear this.

With another smile she prompted her "So there are three ghosts here Rada? Please do tell me all you know!"

To receive another of Rada's gift from the goddess smiles in return, Andie's heart involuntarily missed another beat. Rada exclaimed "Yes, three ghosts Miss Valentine! I feel it is easier to explain to you where we witness all of the action in the exact locations that they happen, rather than attempting to describe rooms you have never ever seen!" Rada added "But first I show you a video on my laptop of the shadow figure I capture on CCTV in the corridor right outside my office door!"

There was a soft knock on the door, making both women jump. Already up on her feet to fetch her laptop from off her desk, Rada opened the door. Claudia smiled at Andie as she set a tray with two coffees on the low metal table positioned a metre or so in front of the sofa. Andie smiled back and stated "Thanks Claudia" She replied in a strong Liverpool accent "You're welcome gorgeous!" Absently rubbing her hand across her buzzed bleached blonde hair, Claudia turned to address Rada "Me shift just ended boss, if there's nothing else, Sammy-Jayne is all alone in me bed at home waiting!" Rada Kostović laughed "Nothing else Claudia, you must not be keeping Sammy-Jayne waiting a second longer! See you again on Friday morning" They watched moments later Claudia literally sprint into the staff car park, dive into the Audi Cabrio, wave at them and without wasting time lowering the roof, depart in a flurry of wheelspin home into the arms of her lover.

Claudia Augello happens to be the grandchild of 1960's super-spy Contessa Marino. Yes, *that* Contessa Marino! The same one who worked alongside Bernice Hampson-Smith, bringing crime-lords and other nefarious villains to justice. Claudia Augello is a rich woman. She works in Kostović because she enjoys interacting with people but mainly as it staves off the boredom. Claudia's illustrious grandmother and her crime fighting partner will get their story told. When the world is ready and the baddies they brought to justice (and their associates!) are no longer able to inflict grievous bodily harm on account of all being long deceased!

*****

Returning to the sofa with her laptop, Rada carefully moved the table nearer and sat next to Andie, she placed it on the low table next to the coffee tray. Playing a video, she froze it after twenty seconds and declared, pointing with the perfectly psychedelic little finger of her left hand at halfway down the screen "Do you also see a shadow figure Miss Valentine? I see it by that door leading down to the cellar. What do you think?" CCTV footage showed a misty cloud drifting through the door they'd passed on the way to her office, Andie replied "I see it Rada! Rare to capture shadow figures on-camera and it's really clear" Delighted with Andie's expert approval, Rada's face was a veritable picture of happiness.

*****

As they drank their coffee, Andie felt the need to tell Rada something "Rada, please don't call me Miss Valentine. My sister Teri and I were born to two movie obsessed parents! I'm after Andie McDowell, for the reason they watched one of her films on their first date and Teri, she's after Teri Hatcher for the spy movie she appeared in and was on in the background as they were making her. Miss Valentine makes me feel I ought to be teaching at some primary school!" They laughed together. "I'm Andie on my channel and to friends, which I think now includes you Rada. Never call me fricking Ghost Babe or we'll be having a serious falling out!" Andie laughed, she received one of Rada's gift from the goddess smiles in response. Andie Valentine found being the recipient of one of Rada Kostović's smiles extremely pleasurable indeed and she wondered if the woman knew how warm and fuzzy deep inside they made her feel.

"There is oat milk in my coffee Rada?" Andie asked, by way of distracting herself away from her own reverie. Rada answered "Yes Andie, Kostović is the entirely vegan bar and restaurant, naturally as sustainable as possible too. This sofa we sit upon is vegan leather. Do you enjoy your coffee?" Andie said "My parents own a bistro and I've tasted oat milk before when I waitressed for them a few years back. Customers ordered their coffee with oat milk, and so I tried one for myself on my break. I honestly think I preferred oat to dairy Rada!" Her gift from the goddess smile illuminated her face "I make the vegan out of you yet Ands! You're okay with me calling you Ands, erm Ands? I just get, your parents, they own Valentine's in Chester, yes? Oh my gosh, I am finding it difficult to concentrate sitting this close by you Ands, you are far too distracting!" Rada giggled.

Andie responded "Yeah Rada, I'm totally cool with Ands. Yeah Rada, you're right about Valentine's" She laughed "I'm sure you're joking with me Rada about finding me distracting. I'm a girl who makes her films, and that's all there is to me. I'm honestly introverted to my core Rada, even if I probs come across like this fricking extroverted gothic film maker! I'm confident talking on-camera, I've been doing this four years and I instinctively get what I need to say, but off-camera I'm kind of quiet. Teri swears I'm possessed by The Morrigan when I'm on-camera and transmogrify into this kind of 'creature'!" Rada giggled "I well know of The Morrigan, I watch every single of your films Ands, perhaps your Teri, she has most valid point!" Andie laughed.

They glanced at one another; their eyes slowly wandered over their dramatically contrasting personal styling. One boho hippie and a goth giggled in mutual amusement. "I like crystals Rada, if they're black!" Andie declared; Rada replied "I own a black dress Ands, it is for if I ever attend funerals!" They collapsed into fits of laughter.

After they'd finished laughing and drinking their coffee, Rada declared "Let's go and explore, Ands!" Placing her laptop back on her desk, she proffered her right hand to Andie "I show you where the ghosts at Kostović hang-out" Andie took a hold of Rada's proffered hand but still raised herself up off the sofa.

From holding her hand, Rada's energy felt as lovely and calm as the woman herself. Andie would gladly have kept holding her hand for the entirety of their walkabout of Kostović to experience more of Rada's chilled-out energy, she reluctantly gave it her back once she'd stood up.

"You're okay me filming our walkthrough Rada?" Andie asked. Rada put her arm across Andie's shoulders "This is so exciting for me, I cannot describe. Oh my gosh! Yes, of course, you must film, perhaps some footage with me in makes it into your video. I make wish to Aphrodite" Rada closed her eyes for a minute "There, it must be so!"

Andie liked Rada. She thought she was far away with the fairies, yet kind of cool. Andie was about to discover Rada had only been warming up so far…

4

Andie filmed on her micro camera "I'll take you to my cellars first Ands, where there are no rodents only ghosts! I watch you react to rats; you do not seem to enjoy them or are your deafening screams in your films just for your audiences? I think you'll sense why we start in cellars, as we explore. I give you the details I am able, then you're conversant with all I know for your investigation" Rada said. Andie replied "Argh, rats freak me out! Everything on Valentine's Night Ghosts happens for real, including my ear-melting screams if I encounter rats! Totally cool of you to share everything you know Rada, and trust me, this isn't always the case, erm, on a case!" They laughed.

They left her office and stood together outside the door, looking down the short corridor at the cellar door "Shall we Ands?" Rada asked "Let's do this Rada!" She replied, they walked in-step towards where the video showed a shadowy mist.

"Do you mind if we stay here a few moments before you open the door Rada?" Andie asked her new friend. Rada replied "This is fascinating and honestly I cannot quite believe here I am beside gorgeous Andie Valentine for her daylight walk-through of my haunted restaurant. Oh my gosh Andie!" Who smiled at her enthusiasm. Rada asked "Please share to me everything you are feeling Ands" She replied "Something powerful likes to leave the cellar and roam in other areas of the building Rada" She gestured for Rada to type in the passcode to unlock the door. Andie pointed her camera away from the door.

"Zero four zero seven" She told Andie "I really tried not to notice Rada, but I couldn't help myself! If I use any of this footage I'll edit this bit out" She laughed, Rada said "You will be needing them when you are down here all alone Ands, of course assuming you do accept my offer of case. The two numbers are the date and month of my birth; I am Cancerian" She informed her. Andie answered "I'm a Piscean" adding "Rada, please do show me every room, then I'll know where to place my fixed cameras and focus all my attention during the investigation" Rada beamed delightedly at Andie with her gift from the goddess smile, she would be professionally returning to Kostović!

"The lights are movement sensitive; there is an over-ride switch in this first room to the left" They'd walked down a wooden flight of stairs and stood in a well-lit corridor. Andie asked her "Please show me this room first Rada, I don't want bright lights illuminating me throughout my investigation!" Once more Rada's gift from the goddess smile came Andie's way, she led their way into said room. Walls painted with bright whitewash and the floor stone flagged, as Andie would soon discover, so was the rest of the cellar, significantly apart from one room.

As per usual Andie Valentine had a sixth sense about the spirits she would be meeting in these cellars, and one in particular rang inner alarm bells in her head. She knew they must investigate every room during their daytime walk-through for a complete picture of the hauntings.

"All the beer in those kegs, it is organic and vegan Ands. Once we leave here, we'll visit the wine cellar next " The room had a lowish ceiling, five foot nine Rada crouched down slightly to prevent snagging her hair on the rough plasterwork above them.

The beer room felt claustrophobic and noisy with all the pumps taking it up the bar in full operation, not the kind of place where anyone would wish to linger for too long. "The control panel is there Ands!" Rada spoke into her ear, even her raised voice still sounded gently soothing, as she pointed with the psychedelic little finger of her right hand at an electrical control panel, She explained all "When we have our annual electrical check, the engineer needs to be able to turn off the electrics in the cellars for testing, he installed by-pass. Andie, this switch labelled lights is the one you want" Andie giggled "You know Rada, I figured out all by myself the light switch was the very one I need!" Rada laughed

"Apologies to you Ands, I know I've got a habit of pointing out the obvious!"

They left the challenging environment of the beer room. Andie turned off her camera, as she waited outside the thankfully closed door for Rada, who was occupied with a call on her phone, speaking in her native tongue. After she'd finished, she told Andie "My mum says Hi to you Ands, I texted her you were here as I saw you through the windows doing your due diligence; before making all of my customers stop in mid-drink or forkful of food as you made your most memorable entrance! Mum's followed Valentine's Night Ghosts long as I have. She instructed me to tell you, ti si tako lijepa!" Rada translated "My mum says you are ever so pretty Andie"

Andie Valentine made a kind offer to Rada, and it was a kind offer that under any other circumstances would be absolute last thing she'd ever suggest "Rada, why don't you take a selfie of us together for your mum?" The two women posed cheek to cheek as Rada took selfies "Cool Ands and thank you so much babes!" Rada sent them off to her mum, who a few seconds later texted back "Dvije prekrasne žene!" Rada was about to translate "Yeah, I get it Rada, please tell your mum thanks from me and how I agree that her daughter is beautiful!" Andie declared. A puzzled expression momentarily crossed Rada's face, her delighted gift from the goddess smile appeared and never had it seemed so radiant. In her

42

softest, most gentle voice, Rada Kostović admitted "Oh my gosh Ands, I forget how I respond in the English; Aphrodite please help me! Erm, thanking you very much for saying this Andie! Goddess Aphrodite is always there for me" Andie stated "Freyja" Offering no further explanation. Rada registered this and said "I texted mum and tell her what you said babes, I too requested she now leaves us to investigate. I'll show you next the wine cellars!"

"Rada, I'll confess all before we get onto the wine cellars, the smell of beer makes me feel sick!" Rada surprised her by placing her right hand on her arm, and sharing "I then also confess Ands, I only drink red wine, and I too dislike the smell and cannot tolerate the taste of beer!" Curious, Andie asked "Any favourite red wine, Rada?" Taking her hand off her arm, she stated "Saint-Émilion Claret Ands, this is the only wine for me in all honesty. I don't stock in Kostović but order it in directly from the vineyard for my personal use; it is of course vegan and organic!"

Andie Valentine experienced goosebumps, she was quite the expert when it came to Saint-Émilion Claret, and she knew for a fact there were literally two vineyards in the entire Bordeaux region where Rada could buy it directly specifically vegan and organic. Andie decided best not to 'go there' right now, responding "Yeah, I enjoy that one too Rada"

*****

Andie turned her micro camera back on. As they walked, Rada began sharing her knowledge of the history "The building itself dates back to 1820, it was always a pub or tavern, originally called The Coach and Horses, known by many names after this, of course I changed the name once again after I bought this run-down building three years ago Ands" Andie asked "Are there any defining moments you know of from the history babes?"

They organically began sometimes referring to each other as babe or babes. It's an English thing generally adopted by young women. Instead of endlessness repeating their first names during conversations, they use babe or babes.

Rada shared some information turning out to be a game-changer on this investigation "From 1840 to about 1860, alongside running as a pub, this building served as the assizes or court covering the area of Liverpool from Bold Street up to Lime Street station; The five cells for anyone awaiting trial exist down here today Ands, we use two of these as our wine cellars! This is a defining moment, yes Ands? Great info, yes?" Rada obviously wanted Andie's validation. Andie declared "Yes, it's amazing info babes!" Rada immediately enveloped her in a delighted hug. She smelled quite exquisite.

"Do you happen to know whereabouts in the building this court was Rada?" Andie asked "The room up on the first floor we use for functions, we may go there next if you wish?" Rada replied, Andie agreed "Yeah, once we're all done exploring down in your claustrophobic cellars, the space and light of this function room of yours sounds perfect Rada!"

*****

Rada announced "We arrive at the cells babes; we go into our red wine cellar first. There's a room down here I don't usually go in Ands, the energy feel too off to me; let's save that until last!" Intrigued, Andie followed Rada into the first of what would turn out to be identical small rooms, this one replete with wine racks containing red wine. The next room the same, white wine filled the shelves. These rooms were again whitewashed, with the flagged floor; guarding each room stood solid oak doors, lacking locks nowadays, but obviously contemporaneous to when they were used as cells.

They entered and exited two more former cells, used for general storage. In the fifth empty and final room Andie stood stock still on the middle with her eyes closed "Ahh, that's interesting, a fixed camera goes in here Rada!" The woman stared wide eyed at Andie "How is this room so interesting Ands? Please share what you feel babes!" She replied "Nothing but residual in all of

45

the other cells, but there's definitely a male spirit in this room, Rada. I won't explore any further right now, I'll wait to uncover what I may during my investigation" Rada glanced around the space "Maybe I imagine Ands, I swear I too feel this ghost in here!" Andie nodded "I trust in what you're sensing is real babes. The male spirit in here is not the one I'm really seeking out, naturally he too deserves fully investigating" Rada looked confused "Andie, honestly I sense this spirit!" Andie smiled and said almost as softly and gently as the woman herself "Rada, I do believe you are psychic!" She followed Rada back out into the corridor.

Seeming unsettled, Any declared "I am now calling upon Hera to protect Andie Valentine and me! Ands, I would not usually evoke Hera. My Goddess is lovely Aphrodite, but Hera protects us when we need her. I show you the creepy room with the nasty spirit! The room always I am avoiding!" She gestured for Andie to lead the way down the narrower passage leading off from the main corridor. Andie Valentine anticipated and already knew the type of experience awaiting them.

Despite the wall mounted motion detecting lights doing their thing, the passage was dark and oppressive. Unlike the rest of the basement complex it smelled damp, and coldness felt like it physically touched their faces as they walked. Halfway down Andie stopped, outlined to the right, ghostly in the bare bricks on the wall, was all that remained of a once stone staircase. Rada explained "Ands, we're directly under where the original main bar would have once been, these were likely steps the landlord used to bring fresh barrels up to his bar" Andie appeared lost in thought, but answered "Hmm, sounds feasible babes, those stairs we used down to get down here are far newer" Rada replied "For sure Ands, there were unsafe wooden steps in the same place when I take over the place, those we came down I got built as part of my renovations of the building"

They entered into this large room with a peculiar layout, the floor in there was dirt and the walls bare bricks, over in one corner stood an alcove, incongruously appearing like some ancient built-in wardrobe, but without any door. Andie Valentine went into the cellars to seek a portal for negative paranormal activity happening in the building, she'd arrived at her destination and she knew it!

Rada shivered "Ooh, Andie I do not enjoy this room at all, this is only fourth time I enter. I am in here now because I needed to show you and I feel safer protected by Hera!" Hearing this, and witnessing for herself how destressed Rada obviously was, Andie decided to expose her to this area for the absolute minimum amount of time "Another fixed camera goes in here Rada, I'll explain later. Okay, let's go!" She guided Rada by her hand out of the creepy room they'd spent less than a minute exploring. Letting go of Rada's hand, she quickly led them along the cellar corridors, up the wooden staircase out of there. She firmly closed the door behind them.

Andie turned off her micro camera for now.

5

Andie needed a conversation with Rada away from the possibility of spirits being able to eavesdrop "After that dark cellar I would enjoy some fresh air. Babes, is there somewhere we can go outside but that's away from the smokers stood around the door? No offence intended if you're a smoker, the stench makes me gag!" Rada's gift from the goddess smile "I've never even tried smoking Ands. My father is a cardiologist, alike my beloved late grandfather. Dad, I am sure would immediately disown Nika, my twin sister and me, if we ever were smoking!" Rada giggled, abd Andie laughed "Are Nika and you identical twins babes?" Rada took out her phone and showed her a photo of them together Andie declared "Oh my gosh! As you'd say Rada. Apart from Nika's hairstyle you're like totally indistinguishable!" Rada's photograph showed the twins chilling by a swimming pool wearing identical summer dresses. Nika's blonde hair was cut into a chin-length bob. Rada shared "Nika works as, how you say the words in English babes, the person who is creating all the clothing for the actors in films?" Andie suggested "Costume designer?" Rada's gift from the goddess smile "Da Ands! Nika works as a costume designer. We're very attuned babes, we sense if the other feels happy, sad or in love without needing to talk. My twin feels as I do and vice versa! Nika, she loves her boyfriend and although yet I need to meet him, strongly I feel this!"

Mentioning being in love made Andie wonder if Rada had any special human in her life; surmising anyone so gorgeous and lovely to be around surely must have. She pondered how any person waking up seeing Rada before anything else was extremely blessed.

*****

"Let's walk around the back and sit in my car for a while Ands and we talk" Rada suggested. They exited through the main bar. Rada clicked on her remote, and the lights on a new style Volkswagen Beetle flashed back. The once lime Beetle completely covered in gorgeous hand painted flowers, psychedelic fractals and peace symbols!

"Fricking, oh wow!" Declared Andie, adding "Rada, your car is the coolest thing ever!" Rada did the introductions "Andie Valentine, please meet Artemis The Beetle!" She responded "Hi Artemis The Beetle!" Rada's gift from the goddess smile appeared, she explained "In times before Kostović, with nothing on one weekend, I go out and buy paint!" Rada drove a car fully expressing her personality, getting Andie's full seal of approval! They entered to sit on hot seats; Rada promptly lowered the windows and welcome fresh air blew across their faces.

"I am sure you wanted this conversation with me away from Kostović and then all the spirits cannot overhear us Ands" Rada stated. From her position in the passenger seat of her car, Andie briefly bowed her head in respect and smiled; with her intuitive way of running her life, she got why Kostović functioned so well, the entire place was one extension of Rada's lovely crazy personality! "Yeah, hundred percent correct babes. With what I know about the entity in that creepy room, no way we could share a one to one anywhere in there!"

"Please tell me all you sensed Ands and what you hope to capture on the fixed camera in that most creepy room" She wondered how much to tell Rada, after all she spent her working life managing the bar containing the nasty spirit that roamed the building, she decided on openness. Anyway she sensed Rada already knew the answer to her questions "The entity in there is unpleasant, intelligent and fully aware of us babes. My fixed camera might not capture anything, but that isn't always why I place them in paranormal hot spots! Talking into my fixed camera frees me up from needing to film on my hand-held, and in locations I know are active this proves useful time after time. I don't know if you've got a plan about what you want me to do, like in terms of clearing any ghosts in Kostović for you Rada, but in my professional opinion that spirit needs dealing with!"

Rada stayed silent, deeply lost within her own thoughts, eventually "Originally, I was going to ask you not to go near any of spirits with the exorcism babes. Encounters with ghosts at Kostović, they'll get shared on our social media and keep customers coming through door to see if they too experience any ghostly encounter. When you are done investigating, if you find there are really the three ghosts here, including that nasty one, please leave all the others, but for sure get rid of him for me Andie!" She nodded in her agreement "I will do if I can babes, in all honesty it could be more like a case of confining him just to that one area in the cellar, he's an old spirit and fricking powerful! Maybe I can contain him, but I'm not confident I could banish him, not on my own!" Rada stared at her in shock "He is that strong?" She replied "Yes, he really is" Rada nodded grimly "Please be finding out all you can, but do not be putting yourself in danger Andie; I would never forgive myself if harm came to you in Kostović!" Andie placed her hands together in front of her chest as she bowed her head "Namaste Rada Kostović" Bowing back in response "Namaste Andie Valentine!" They sat smiling at one another.

*****

Silence, comfortable silence, then "I guess you're getting asked this constantly Rada, but I'm too curious. Where abouts in the Balkans are you originally from?" Rada's gift from the goddess smile came Andie's way as she answered "Not asked often as you'd imagine Ands! Many pretend they do not notice I am speaking with an accent, think it wouldn't be woke!" They giggled "I guess they imagine I am unaware I have accent and are concerned they offend me if asking where I originate from!" Andie laughed "Tell me please, gorgeousness!" Rada smiled enigmatically and she answered "I am a Croatian chick from Zagreb originally. I leave my home at eighteen to study Global Ecology and Evolution at University of Liverpool. I adore Liverpool since I learn of it at school, I read all I could find about the city. I decide there is where I'll study. I am passionately Liverpudlian, I never dream to live any place else, I am so deeply in love with this city Ands!"

*****

Rada looked thoughtful while she asked "How come you understand Croatian?" Andie felt compelled to share all her truths with her, instinctively sensing there should be no secrets between them, yet not understanding why.

"I'm a professional violinist and five years ago I toured across the entire Balkans for six months with an orchestra! I'm still in the orchestra and play with them when they tour" Rada looked taken aback "Oh my gosh! I have not the clue about this side of you Ands, yet I suppose this is hardly something you could share on Valentine's Night Ghosts" They giggled.

"Too true Rada 'It's 3am, I begin my solo investigation in this fricking creepy cemetery located on this freaky misty moor thirty miles from civilization, and by the way, I'm a professional violinist' would that work babes?" The two of them found this beyond hilarious and couldn't talk for several minutes.

"How did you learn Croatian Ands, was it as a by-product of hearing it spoken everywhere you travelled?" Andie had never shared any details of the relationship between herself and Candy's drummer with a soul, especially her family, she found the whole episode deeply embarrassing. Andie took a deep breath "I fell into this relationship with the drummer from the orchestra. She was from Belgrade in Serbia. On the tour bus she taught me to speak and read her language. I know Serbian's not identical to Croatian, but it's enough alike to understand your mum's texting. Mila dumped me like literally the night before our tour concluded in her home city! Candy's my musical heroine and the orchestra leader. She confided when we travelled home together, as I cried for the entire journey; Mila was married with two children. I wish she'd decided to share this nugget before I'd fricking slept with the woman!" She added "Mila left the orchestra after that tour, I'd hardly continue playing with them if she hadn't!"

*****

Rada leant across to hug Andie "Hvala vam što ste ovo podijelili. Volim te zbog tvoje iskrenosti!" She stated in her softly gentle voice "You understand?" Andie equally softly replied "Yeah, I understand. If you love my honesty, I love your empathy Rada. I adore this about you!" A van pulled up onto the pavement nearby, the driver jumped out, she smiled over at them and began unloading boxes and taking them in through the rear entrance of the shop next door.

Their spell broken, Andie said "I'm thinking your time is precious Rada, and yet here I am keeping you away from work as you show me around, we should get back inside and continue with your tour!" Rada wore her gift from the goddess smile "Oh my gosh! Yes babes, let us get back inside Kostović"

6

They walked alongside one another into the still packed main bar; multiple pairs of eyes focused on Andie as per usual and also on the smiling boho vision of gorgeousness by her side. It might sound like exaggerating suggesting that the entire clientele of Kostović fell silent at the sight of two highly contrasting women entering the room, yet this isn't too far off what happened.

Andie noticed a large brass sign situated above the fire door on the left-hand wall, stating customers needed to head that way for the toilets, and more relevantly to her, The Coach and Horses Function Suite. Andie liked how Rada kept the original name of Kostović alive with her choice of name for their function room.

Passing through the fire door, they turned sharply to the right and walked past the toilets; another fire door stood before them 'This way to The Coach and Horses Function Suite' was helpfully written on the brass plaque affixed above it. Carpeted stairs led the way to the upper level, Rada informed Andie "That fire door to our right leads eventually back to my office Ands, we used the short-cut through the kitchen when we went there earlier. Babes, the stairs leading up to the function room are in front of us, should we go straight-up or do you want a moment?" Andie replied "Yeah Rada, let's go straight up; share all you know of the history once we're up there" Rada's gift from the goddess smile confirmed she would.

Passing through fire doors after ascending the stairs, one short corridor later and the sign announced The Coach and Horses Function Suite awaited their arrival, through yet more fire doors!

Before they entered, Rada explained "This room needed to be soundproofed. We hire it for all types of functions; there could be a band playing or DJing happening. Our customers down in the main bar should be able to enjoy their drink and meal in peace. All the doors are only part of the soundproofing; underneath the floor we too have sound-deadening. The most we ever hear downstairs is a kind of distant noise of party, but it is never intrusive"

On her cases Andie Valentine is focussed on getting told facts relevant to her paranormal investigation; she's not in the slightest bit interested in listening to anything else about her client. Naturally, there have been occasions a client considered Andie a rude young woman, especially when holding up her hand signalling for them to desist telling her anything not pertinent to her investigation!

Throughout her four years investigating the paranormal there were two exceptions to her rule. Firstly she met Zen Sanders, their mutual raw lust ensured he captured her full attention. And then Andie had met Rada Kostović. She found the woman relaxingly lovely to be around. Andie thoroughly respected her and genuinely listened as Rada talked her through the technicalities of sound-proofing her function room!

*****

They simultaneously pushed open the double fire doors to enter the next area of Andie's ghost tour of Rada's bar.

Fully carpeted in deepest blue, a dance floor dominated a third of the floor space, behind which stood the smallish stage. Tables and chairs took up the other two thirds of the room. A miniature bar situated on the same wall as the entrance doors, through a swing door adjacent to the bar was a kitchen. Andie's intuition told her not to enter into the kitchen yet, feeling this would prove relevant during the investigation, she chose to leave it unexplored.

Rada pointed with the little finger of her right hand at the wall behind the bar and announced "I think you will find this interesting Ands, on the wall over there is the old oil painting, we find it in cellars during renovation, it shows how this room looked back when it was the assizes!"

They went together behind the bar to take a closer look. Court was in session, the judge sat on his dais, clearly in exactly the same location as the stage on the other side of the room, the unfortunate defendant looking nervous in the dock awaited his fate. The usual crowd of interested onlookers packed the public gallery. Some of the fixtures and fitting illustrated in this two centuries old piece of art were evident today. Wooden shutters on the inside of the windows and the same beams spanning the ceiling.

"For about twenty years this room was used for passing of the judgement, beginning in around 1840. Thankfully for Kostović the guilty were not hung here, but rather at the official location for public executions. When it's quiet in here I swear I am hearing the judge condemning souls for their crimes. I wonder how many convicted commit crimes by our modern ethic? Please say something Ands!" Rada stared at her anxiously, since taking in the details of the oil painting, Andie Valentine stood still with her eyes closed.

"Apologies babes, I promise I heard everything you said. After absorbing the contents of the painting, I attempted to superimpose the details into the room before us now, I'll admit not successfully, but during my investigation I feel this will be a different matter"

She added "Talking of which Rada, I need to ask you the obvious question. Kostović is open from eleven in the morning until midnight all weekdays and much later on Saturday. You know the way I work babes. I'm going to need the entire building to myself!" Rada's gift from the goddess smile "Andie, I follow Valentine's Night Ghosts for four years, if anyone knows how you are working on a case, it's the chick right in front of you! Already I think muchly about this, are you available for the evening of Monday next week?" If Andie wasn't, she now would be "Da Rada, I'm available on Monday next" Rada smiled "Excellent to hear Ands! Kostović will all be closed from 4pm onwards on that Monday, we'll allow for cleaners to do their stuff, let's say we meet in here again at six o'clock on the Monday, 4th August, does that sound good Ands?" Andie thought this sounded extremely good "Awesome Rada! How long do I get for my investigations babes?" Rada replied "Please be taking exactly as long as you are needing" Andie smiled at her.

"I hope you understand that we cannot go to the main bar to discuss your investigation in there. I live up on the top floor Ands, do you feel okay with going upstairs to my apartment to continue on with our conversation?" Andie replied "Yeah…" getting interrupting mid-sentence; they were opening the fire doors to leave when a loud sound came from behind the bar!

They glanced briefly at one another, and as one sprinted back into the room and to straight behind the bar. An unbroken bottle of beer lay right in the middle of the floor gently rocking from side to side. They'd been in that exact same location two minutes earlier and there was certainly no beer bottle on the floor then. Rada casually picked it up and placed it back on the shelf with its friends.

Apparently unperturbed, Rada declared "Ands, I almost forget to tell you this, I am most glad we returned to the room! There is the cushion on a chair over here, look I'll show you" They walked across the dance floor to a large table with eight chairs. She pointed with the psychedelic little finger of her left hand "I have not witnessed this for myself, but many customers claim how the cushion of this chair, it is going down alike someone is sat there babes!" Andie replied "Thanks Rada, now I know this, I'll place a fixed camera right here!"

7

"You appeared totally unphased by the flying beer bottle Rada, is that kind of phenomena happening constantly in Kostović?" Andie asked her, as they finally left The Coach and Horses Function Suite.

Rada stopped walking and turned to face Andie "Babes, I may not be an expert on the paranormal like you, yet I am watching hundreds of hours of your videos in these four years. Yes Andie, to be answering your question, all the time it happens! Aside from that scary room in my cellar, through following you for so long I am not afraid usually; and also especially I need to be setting the good example to my staff. If I seem unconcerned, they won't be either"

Andie felt moved her work had so informed Rada's life. Clearing her throat, she said "Shall we?" Gesturing for them to continue walking again. They went back down to the ground floor and entered the corridor Rada stated earlier led the long way back to her office. Immediately upon entering the corridor, another security protected door stood to the right "When is the date of your birthday Ands?" Andie replied "6th March, why?" Rada explained "Zero six zero three. I change the security code daily Ands. Today is your birthday!" Andie giggled at Rada's joke.

The door opened to reveal an elevator "We also could go via fire escape in our car park, I feel this way is kinder to you in those boots Ands" Andie laughed "Thanks!"

They exited the lift straight into what appeared to be an artist's studio. Rada said "Always I dream of my own art studio and when I decide I'll live above Kostović, this is room I specify first and then everything else. Although it was last area of renovation to get completed. There is no, how you say, sitting room. My studio, kitchen, bathroom and the bedroom, this is all I ever needed babes!" Walls were all in natural brick, the floor pine and six windows ensured plenty of natural daylight. Andie gazed around herself in awe, taking in all of Rada's incredible studio! Completed artworks stood up against the walls, gorgeous fantasy art. Aside from Rada's easel, the only furniture consisted of one futon covered with Mondrian style fabric and a table in front of it, also in a classic Mondrian pattern. Andie finally found her voice "Rada, your studio is like incredible!!! I adore everything you painted! Oh wow, it's a magical place in here babes!"

Wearing her gift from the goddess smile, Rada kicked off her sandals, pirouetted ballet style, hitching up the skirt of her long dress, she proceeded to dance gracefully three times around her entire studio, stopping in front of Andie. Taking Andie's hands in hers, she leant in towards her and whispered in her ear "I adore you love it, Andie!" and suggested "Let's go to sit in my kitchen,

I'll make us coffee" Rada stared expectantly at Andie waiting for her answer, she smiled at Rada; this inspired or just plain crazy idea had entered her head. Of course, instantly Andie decided to act upon it!

*****

"Before you make coffee, I want to show you something Rada. If I went out dressed like this every day I'd go mad from getting stopped every hundred metres by followers. Of course, I love them to bits, yet all of their attention gets intrusive. I've decided to show you the way I'm usually looking every day Rada. Have you a dress petite enough I may borrow off you please? I promise I'll return it when I see you next Monday and obviously washed. What size shoes are you babes?" Rada seemed intrigued "There is a dress I own too small on me, yet maybe not too big on you. Size five shoes, and this is alike you is it not, yes?" Andie replied "Thanks Rada! Yeah, I'm also a five"

Carrying her make-up removing wipes, a white bandana, her borrowed dress and flat vegan hemp sandals, Andie entered Rada's bathroom, firmly closing the door behind her. First she removed her contact lenses...

She emerged twenty minutes later to the delicious aroma of fresh ground coffee. Following the scent, Andie found Rada Kostović in full barista mode in her kitchen "Hello babe" Andie announced her arrival. Rada turned around, her mouth fell open in shock "Poop Andie, you are so tiny! Apologies, never normally I am this crude! Andie, not any chance I recognise you if I did not already know that is you! Literally not one single thing looks alike the famous Valentine's Night Ghosts investigator. As I thought, that white gypsy dress fits better you than me, it is now yours! You are beautiful but in utterly different way! Already I am decided Andie, I prefer A-Natural to A-Goth in all of the honesty. I adore you as hippie chick alike me" Andie laughed "Thanks Rada, there's no need to apologise for saying poop and I already know how fricking small I am!" Rada giggled and hugged Andie.

*****

They sat opposite each other at Rada's rustic kitchen table, in her authentically rustic kitchen, enjoying coffee. Andie asked "Please share everything that happens in the main bar Rada" The woman answered "It feels so weird talking to you suddenly alike different woman in my apartment! Your glasses are lovely on you Andie! Oh my gosh, I only just noticed your eyes are sapphire! Why you hide those gorgeous eyes with tinted contact lenses?" Andie replied "I like them Rada. I can barely see a thing without lenses or glasses! Please tell me everything about your main bar" Rada leant back in her chair "Okay, in main bar babes, we have got glasses flying, alike the bottle we saw ourselves upstairs and they never break, hundreds have witnessed this, my staff and customers, undoubtedly this is reality. People are getting gently touched on their elbows, and yet sometimes they are scratched down the middle of their back. Yes Andie, the three scratches like a demon makes, for sure you are about to be asking me this question, yes?"

Andie Valentine giggled "You truly have watched all of my videos Rada! You know better than me what I'm about to ask you next! How frequently do these events occur and is there anything different happening in other parts of the building. Oh, also is there any pattern to them or are they like random events?"

Rada answered "Maybe once a week, then there are times when it is for sure far more active with the stuff and it's like every single day, and then pft! Nothing for months and here we are thinking perhaps it is finito; suddenly a dramatic event occurs and we get back to the square one again. It is the main bar we see most stuff, but then it is always occupied, there might be stuff happening in my cellars or up in the function room constantly but nobody is there to witness. I think there's pattern Ands, the week of the full moon more occurs, and the spirits seem more active in Autumn. Of course, it is obvious why full moon make the spirits active. Also, some customers experience painful headaches, this happens with me too a few times, as quickly as the headache arrives, it goes. Is it that creepy cellar spirit the one doing all the scratching and causing these headaches Ands? Oh, I nearly forgot to ask you, I sense nothing ghostly or negative in my apartment, am I correct in this babes?"

Andie Valentine doesn't speculate too much before her investigation, she prefers to keep an open mind "Until I investigate I couldn't categorically say the scratchies are down to him babes, what I got from our walkthrough is there are more than three spirits frequenting Kostović. My task on the night is to make sense of everything and if I may, put names to these spirits. I'll need to determine if their interactions with the living is seeking attention or something far more sinister! Hundred percent agree with you Rada about your apartment, I've been in here for like two hours and sensed ništa paranormal!"

Rada's gift from the goddess smile "This is making me wish I could investigate with you, but I am thinking how I would likely get in the way more than be of the help to you" She laughed. Andie replied "In all seriousness, I'm likely to be messing things up in here pretty badly on the Monday night! Like I mentioned, our nasty friend in the cellar is powerful and needs containing. Under any other circumstances I'd be delighted to have you as my guest co-investigator Rada. What's more, you know exactly the way I work during my investigation; however in this case I couldn't guarantee your safety"

Rada looked her in the eyes "Andie, I work here, likely I am spending more time down there, than I am all alone up in my apartment!" Rada gestured around her "I am not a little girl; I do not need protecting by you or anyone else babe. The only part of investigation I admit scares the blinking living daylights out of me is that creepy room in my cellar! Please agree to having me with you Andie, for sure protect me creepy room every of your powers! At all other times I take of care of myself with the help of my Goddess Aphrodite, as always I am doing. I badly want to investigate along with you Andie, please allow me on this case with you!" Rada lowered her head, opening her pale blue eyes wide, gazing up at Andie in appeal.

Rada Kostović's lusciousness, staring appealing up into Andie's eyes was truly something to behold! Anyone in possession of a pulse facing this lovely hippie gazing at them the same way, doesn't matter male or female, gay or straight, they would find it impossible to refuse her wish.

Naturally, Andie relented "Okay Rada, we'll investigate Kostović together; all being well we'll reach the end with our sanity intact!" She added "The film I'll make of this case is going to get seen by millions on Valentine's Night

Ghost, sure you're okay with that babes?" Rada couldn't have looked happier "To be featured on your channel is my dream of four years Andie, of course I am okay with this and now I cannot wait until Monday evening! Do I need a meditation or anything else in the readiness for our investigation?" Andie Valentine smiled "If you feel it'll help, yeah do a meditation. As you've seen, I even do this occasionally during an investigation seeking a few extra insights. My advice is keep an open mind and obviously feel free to talk on-camera whenever you want"

"I have an idea for what I'll wear as investigation outfit, are you okay with me in a crimson mini dress Andie? You usually wear dresses, yet I do not copy your style. I am not goth. Are you nowadays just gothic only on camera?" Andie was extremely okay with the prospect of Rada in a crimson mini dress, she imagined Rada would look quite lovely! She answered "Although I don't externalize as I used to; I'm always a goth inside me Rada! Please feel free to wear whatever you want, feeling comfortable matters most, if you feel you should wear that dress babes, then of course you must do!"

It was at this moment Rada's comment 'I am all alone up in my apartment' finally registered with Andie Valentine. She giggled as she said "Rada Kostović, you're a lovely person and a gorgeous woman but freaking crap balls I wouldn't compete against you at

69

poker, you're way too good. You'll always get precisely what you want babes!"

Rada gazing steadily into Andie eyes, blessing her with a radiant gift from the goddess smile, declaring "A-Natural, volim te!"

*****

It might seem like Rada manipulated Andie to become a part of her investigation, yet in all fairness this wouldn't be telling the entire story. Rada Kostović was aware of karmically exactly who and what Andie Valentine was in relation to her, although the woman herself was oblivious to the any of that at this point.

LOOK INTO THE WINDOWS OF MY SOUL
As I gaze into the windows of your soul
Oneness reflected
PART TWO

1

Monday 4th August saw Andie double-checking cameras and all her ghost-hunting equipment, charging-up extra battery packs and eating typically lightly.

Kostović would be her first investigation since Zen Sanders and her had parted ways. The prospect of investigating solo scared her; she'd got used to talking to her co-investigator, and although they had only worked together for ten months, not having the security blanket of someone else to play-off and against made her feel uncomfortable. She felt grateful that Rada would be there beside her, although inexperienced, Andie sensed she wouldn't require any babysitting.

Andie Valentine was aware how unfair it was to compare; yet this didn't stop her doing precisely that...

Experienced Zen Sanders knew the protocols of going out on paranormal investigations for long before they'd met. After all, he'd been investigating the paranormal for ten years, his preferred locations London's derelict buildings. An urban explorer, he'd never cared about the formality of getting official permission. Demon obsessed Zen also crucially knew how to remain safe from possible psychic attacks, allowing him to provoke and generally wind-up demonic entities without too much risk of attachments or fear of serious harm befalling him. She used to joke with Zen how demons were scared of him!

Rada Kostović wasn't an experienced ghost hunter, and yet Andie conceded she shared her bar with many spirits and to the best of her knowledge, the worse attacks she'd experienced were those headaches. Andie knew those are commonplace on paranormal investigations from psychic feedback. Even she wasn't immune!

She would later discover Rada's headaches weren't from psychic feedback, but something altogether nastier.

Considering the psychic portal Rada Kostović worked in, Andie wondered how she'd remained free of anything more invasive affecting her. She knew Rada was psychic; after all she'd intuitively felt that first ghost in the cellar and sensed that the other room was a place she needed to avoid. Rada was aware meditating before investigations helps the psychic remain centred.

*****

Having a few days to ponder over everything and watch back through her footage, these are the conclusions Andie reached about Kostović.

The cellars would be their first area of investigation. She wanted to communicate with the spirit located in the cell room to learn more about him. Inevitably also the creepy spirit would definitely require dealing with, but figured she'd cross that bridge when she arrived at it!

Secondly, they'd investigate the function room. She kept her usual open mind about what they'd discover in there, yet instinct told her there would likely be a poltergeist.

Thirdly, their investigation in the main bar, where Andie wanted to try out some kit she'd never used before. This was not without risks, however given the vastness of the location, Andie figured why the heck not?

With her equipment passing her scrutiny, and six fully charged extra battery packs ready to use as required, she went about, what to her was the pleasant task of neatly packing it into two of her aluminium wheely cases.

Andie was ready. Having already established from Rada; Claudia didn't have any shifts earlier that week, and she could use her parking place on the staff car park; Andie loaded her cases into the back of Scorpy.

She texted Rada, letting her know she was setting off and then pulled out of her yard. Thirty minutes later, as Andie queued to pay her toll to drive through the Queensway Mersey Tunnel, she sent Rada another message, letting her know she'd be arriving in fifteen minutes. She felt a tingle of excitement about a new case and at the prospect of spending an entire evening in Rada's lovely energy.

2

Rada Kostović was used to feeling empowered. After all, this is the woman who'd taken a run-down old pub and armed only with her vision for what she could make it, transformed it into one of the go-to places for vegans to hang-out and dine-out in Liverpool. Monday morning Rada felt nervous, far more nervous than she would care to admit.

Once she discovered that Zen Sanders was no longer on the scene; Rada saw an opportunity to fulfil karmic destiny; a small part of which was investigating alongside Andie in her own bar and restaurant.

This didn't stop the butterflies in her stomach, together with an overwhelming feeling of unease about what lay before her. At 4pm, as she locked the doors to customers, bidded her staff an early goodnight and let in the cleaning team eight hours earlier than normal, Rada's hands were actually shaking.

She wasn't in the slightest bit impressed with herself!

She decided she had two hours in which to re-centre and restore her temporarily lost calmness. She went off to her office to meditate for one hour, just about fitting laid out full length on the Chesterfield. She admonished herself to cease immediately being ridiculous and to own her fear, mindfully channelling it to re-empower herself. Naturally she called on Aphrodite to help her.

The second text message arrived from Andie at five forty, letting Rada know she was waiting to pay her toll on the other side of the Mersey to drive through the tunnel. Rada went back to her office for a final communication with herself and Aphrodite. She smiled. After all, she'd sensed this moment would likely arrive for four years. Her inner calmness returned and she smiled again.

Feeling once more like herself, Rada focused her attention on practicalities; deciding where to await for Andie and how she would create the pattern interrupt she knew was necessary for the maximum impact shortly after this. She sensed their investigations would go well; but would feel massively disappointed in herself if she didn't initiate the action needed to allow their karma to align.

Rada Kostović knew she and Andie Valentine had existed throughout other countless previous lives interconnected. She sensed this might be the case watching Valentine's Night Ghosts, since meeting Andie, spending time within her aura and meditating afterwards, Rada was convinced of their karmic destiny.

3

Andie Valentine reversed Scorpy into Claudia's parking place at Kostović at exactly six o'clock, as they'd agreed. Walking around to the front with her two wheely cases, she saw the 'closed' sign on the front door, and strolled on in. Last time she'd been there it had been this hive of activity, that evening it was deserted. No thirsty, hungry customers or busy bar staff attending to their needs.

Rada sat on her favourite bar stool awaiting her arrival. Andie immediately noticed Rada wasn't wearing a mini dress after all, although she looked elegance personified in her lemon maxi dress; she felt slightly disappointed. As before her blonde hair was tied with white ribbons into two plaits.

Taking inspiration from Rada, Andie's hair was in a thick braid down the back. She wore an open backed long black dress. When out on cases she preferred military boots, making no noise as she walked and really comfortable.

Rada stood up as she arrived and walked across to greet her "Very much I admire your styling Ands, you have the great body! I love your tattoo, this is rune for Freyja, yes?" Andie's inking on her lower back was made visible by her open backed dress "First prize goes to the hippie from Liverpool!" Rada giggled; she leant over to kiss Andie twice on both her cheeks in greeting. "Kostović is all quiet just as promised, we are only living souls in entire building Andie!" Rada's exquisite scent pleasantly overwhelmed her senses.

*****

Rada announced "This has been the busiest of days babe; please accept my apologies for not already being ready. Excuse me for just the few minutes, I need to be getting changed and refreshing my make-up" She replied "Yes, of course Rada" Receiving her gift from goddess smile, she added "Help yourself to the coffee Andie, and soon I return!" Andie did exactly that. Sitting herself on Rada's still warm vacated bar stool, she lifted her wheely cases up onto the bar and checked over her equipment one last time.

Andie glanced at the clock up on the wall behind the bar, Rada had been gone for thirty-seven minutes. As she was wondering how it could possibly take Rada that long to simply change her dress, the door of the corridor leading to her apartment opened and Rada made her entrance...

Andie took in the feast for the eyes in her crimson mini dress with red stilettos. Liberated from plaits, luxuriant blonde hair cascaded down her back. She experienced the same shock Rada had when she went 'any-girl' for her.

Rada's plan was fully in action, she'd created the impact she needed, next for the pattern interrupt...

Andie watched wide-eyed as Rada strutted like a model across the room, stopping two metres in front of her. Rada turned her back on her, carefully arranging her hair over her right shoulder and gazing back over her left shoulder at Andie. She lifted her mini dress over her bum revealing a colourful tattoo of a dove on her lower back; she wasn't wearing any underwear. Rada softly declared"Aphrodite, she is with me always; we have the matching tattoos Ands!" Andie finally found her voice "Your tattoo is very beautiful babes!" Rada released her dress. It fell back down to cover her up once more.

They gazed at one another in silent mutual appreciation for what seemed to them like hours but was really only a minute or so. Andie needed to tell her...

"Rada, you're lovely to be around, your personal energy is so beautiful! You're gorgeous Rada and you're a crazy woman who makes me laugh, and I love this about you! I feel like I've known you forever babes"

Rada's gift from the goddess smile lit up her face "Ands, thank you, this mean a lot, especially coming from you! I expressed my appreciation for gift of your beauty soon after we meet, your energy too is lovely to be around. Do you believe in reincarnation?" Andie was getting used to expecting the unexpected from Rada, she replied "Yeah, of course reincarnation is real" Rada smiled, not with her usual gift from the goddess smile, more like the wisdom of countless lifetimes shone through her "Andie, do you know about Twin-Flames? I don't mean the Soulmates, but specifically Twin-Flames" Andie shook her head and said "No Rada, I think I read about them online once, but honestly, I'm not sure exactly what Twin-Flames means" Rada fell silent for a moment.

Rada Kostović was aware that her role was to initiate the action required to fulfil their joint karmic destiny. She now knew Andie Valentine was unaware at this time of Twin-Flames. Rada fully understood Twin-Flames come together when arriving at the upper limit of evolvement possible independently and the legends proclaim Twin-Flames are two separate halves of the one complete soul, remaining individuals, together they make up the two interlocking pieces of one whole soul. Back through time immemorial it has been proclaimed those who are ready will find their long-lost Twin-Flame. Rada knew a Twin-Flame connection is not necessarily as lovers, but rather to learn and evolve, yet it may for sure be physical. Andie looked expectantly at her, waiting for her to explain 'Oh my gosh!' thought Rada, she'd predicted this might be the only way, out loud she said "Aphrodite please reveal all!"

*****

Intentionally staying two metres in front of Andie, and taking in a few deep breaths to calm herself, Rada knew the crucial moment had finally arrived. Feeling almost overwhelmingly vulnerable, almost overwhelmingly yet not quite, she began...

"Do you have a lover?" She asked Andie "No Rada" With this confirmed, Rada asked "You tell me you enjoy my company Andie, this is for sure case, yes?" Her response was "Yeah babe, I think I enjoy your company more than anyone I've ever met" Andie hadn't a clue why she was getting asked these random questions, but she figured it must all be about these Twin-Flames and she'd doubtless explain all soon.

With all that established Rada felt considerably calmer. She let go of personal involvement in the outcome, from now on it was all down to her Aphrodite. She'd no idea what Andie would answer to her next question. "Do you find me attractive Andie? I'll be plain speaking with you, so you're clear what I am asking you. Do you fancy me?" A thoroughly mystified Andie honestly answered "To be just as plain-speaking as you, yeah Rada I fancy you a lot, you're like a living goddess!" Rada's familiar gift from the goddess smile illuminated her face. She exclaimed "Oh my gosh Andie! I too appreciate your beauty, but already I tell you multiple times, surely this you know?!"

Rada asked her the final million-dollar question, the one making her feel uncharacteristically nervous the entire day "If you desire me, I am your girlfriend Andie. Do you desire me?" Andie responded by practically yelling out "Rada, I desire you more than I've ever desired any human being! Fricking yes Rada, please will you be my girlfriend!!!" The sheer intensity of raw passion she'd exhibited responding to Rada's final question even surprised Andie herself!

*****

Pansexual Andie Valentine already planned on asking Rada out on a date after their investigation, although she kind of got all the right signals from her, Andie wasn't totally sure she was even into women. Rada's directness nullified the need for any dates; they were now officially girlfriends!

Rada stepped towards Andie. They kissed. Hand in hand they practically sprinted in the direction of Rada's lift.

FIVE SPIRITS ONE BAR
If these walls could talk
Yet maybe they do
PART THREE

1

They made their way down to film the introduction in the main bar for nine o'clock. They each carried a hand-held camera, although they'd yet to switch them on. Rada now wore her more typical floral maxi dress, her trainers from when they'd first met and underwear! Although her hair remained down and free.

As usual, Andie Valentine filmed her scene-setting intro on a fixed camera, set up on the bar this time. "Welcome to Valentine's Night Ghosts, if you're new to my channel, Hi, I'm Andie Valentine! For this case I'm in one of my favourite cities, Liverpool. The city famous for its music scene, soccer teams and best not forget, the iconic River Mersey! This case features a bar with a difference. Over two centuries old, this popular vegan bar and restaurant is reputedly haunted by at least three spirits! Way back this place was called The Coach and Horses, these days it's known as Kostović" Andie paused a moment "Before my investigation begins, I have news to share; demon expert Zen Sanders has left Valentine's Night Ghosts. I'm sure my subscribers and regular viewers will join with me in thanking Zen Sanders for all that he brought to our cases together. Personally, I thank him unreservedly for the incredible ten months of pushing the envelope on our cases. Zen, I send you my love and good wishes for your future!" She paused again for a moment "I'm not alone for this investigation. It's time to introduce my guest co-investigator for tonight, Rada Kostović. As you may have guessed, Rada also happens to be the owner of Kostović! As it's you who's called me in tonight Rada, please share some of the paranormal events your staff and customers regularly experience in Kostović"

Andie panned her hand-held camera onto Rada "Andie, thank you from bottom of my heart for allowing me to investigate in Kostović with you, it means the world to me; I enjoy watching your cases for four years. To Zen Sanders, I am sending you all my love and wishing you all you desire for your future! Of course, I could never fill the shoes of fearless Zen. I do my best to be inspired by his limitless bravery during my night alongside Andie for Valentine's Night Ghosts"

Rada had brilliantly drawn a line, definitively closing the Zen Sanders era on Valentine's Night Ghosts! Rada added "Andie, in Kostović glasses fly off the shelves, customers are touched on their arms; and get scratched sometimes. When the place is closed, we are hearing noises like an unseen person is walking along our empty corridors. In our cellars Ands, there is a scary spirit!"

Andie declared "I'm looking forward to meeting it!" She asked "How long have you owned Kostović for Rada?" She replied "Three years; it took me half a year before I could open the door to customers!" Andie further asked "What do you know of the history of this building from before you took it over?" Rada's gift from the goddess smile "Much research I did Ands, as I wait for multiple renovations to be completed. I wanted to know every bit of the history I could find! This building dates back to 1820, and as you mentioned, was then called The Coach and Horses. Obviously, then always it was a pub; but for around twenty years it also served as the assizes court, only for the area of Liverpool immediately surrounding it though. Ands, our function room upstairs was where this court used to be, in our cellars were five cells for those awaiting trial. They remain existing to this day!"

Rada asked "Andie, in which order are we investigating tonight?" Smiling, she responded "Rada, first we'll go and explore in your cellars, you mentioned a scary spirit; as I placed fixed cameras in two locations in the cellars, I sensed exactly what you were talking about! It's going to be fascinating to learn more about him. The second of our investigations takes place in the former court, now known as The Coach and Horses Function Suite. And to finish off our investigation for tonight, Rada, we'll return to your main bar; as you're with me and I trust you like family, I plan on attempting The Estes Method, never used this before but it reputedly gives amazing results. I'll explain all later Rada, once we're back in here!"

Rada announced "Please wish us all of your luck, as next we head off to investigate the spirits at Kostović!" Andie turned off her camera "Rada, that was a perfect impro at the end; you're a fricking natural talking to camera; okay babes let's do this!" They set off towards the cellars.

*****

During a brief conversation in Rada's apartment earlier, they'd agreed on how their cellar investigation would all work. They strolled hand in hand the short distance to the cellar door; upon arriving they talked through their plan of action one last time.

Before opening the cellar door, Andie Valentine asked "Rada, you're totally sure you feel okay alone for your investigation in cell five?" Rada looked her levelly in the eyes "Oh my gosh Ands, as long as I am never needing to set my foot into the creepy room, willingly I investigate every single one of cells! Aphrodite, she has my back as always" Andie smiled, she appreciated Rada felt nervous at the prospect of what lay ahead, she reassured her "I've checked your camera; and you have your flashlight and the Spirit Box is with you. We'll walk down to the cellars together and have a conversation on-camera, setting the scene. After that you go off for your solo investigation and I'll go and see what's waiting for me! If you need me for any reason, scream and I'll be right there!" Andie hugged her.

Rada declared "Andie, I cannot believe we investigate together, okay obviously not exactly together, yet I am sure you understand what I mean!" they laughed.

*****

"We're here in the beer pumping room in the vast cellars under this ancient pub. Clearly people two centuries ago were smaller than you Rada! Whilst I'm okay down here, being way too petite for headroom to be like an issue for me, you're really going to need to watch you don't knock yourself out or end up attached by your hair to the ceiling!" They giggled. Rada stated "I am careful always for these issues down here Ands! We are in this odorous beer room as the master light control is located here, I turn off all lights now Ands!" She did just that; they switched their camera's on night vision setting.

Andie said "Let's leave this room Rada and get on with our investigation. We're each going off for a solo vigil in two different rooms in the cellars. With this being such a large building and wanting to investigate as much as we can of Kostović, this is the only way we'll get to cover all the places I feel we should. We'll go firstly to drop Rada off where she's investigating, and after I'll head over to my own solo location"

Turning on their flashlights, as one they gingerly walked along the main cellar corridor, with Rada crouching low to avoid her hair becoming a part of the ceiling.

"These doors we pass on our right, they are former cells from the 19th century. The cell behind this fifth door is where I investigate tonight! I promise I tell you more of the history in there" Rada said this into her hand-held camera, and then it was Andie's turn to speak "Rada, good luck with your investigation, shout out if you need me!" She hugged Rada; doing her level best to make this look professional on-camera, and not at all like Rada was her lover. Unfortunately for Andie, she didn't pull this off terribly well. Professionally she announced "See you later Rada, and like I said, scream or yell if you need any help!" With that said, Andie walked away.

2

As Rada entered cell five and closed the door behind her, she felt above anything grateful at not having to return and explore the creepiest room ever with Ands!

She quietly resolved, unless a ghost was tearing her limb from limb, no way would she be shouting for any help. Rada reasoned it was her own suggestion, each of them doing a solo investigation, and Andie would be having her hands way too full dealing with that scary thing in the creepy room! The last thing Andie needed was getting distracted by a hysterical chick screaming for her help! Rada decided that whatever happened in cell five was all on her and she would just need to be finding some way to deal with this. Rada wore her gift from the goddess smile, first to smooth over the little mess Ands created, and with that done, onto her investigation; she already adored this! Calling on Aphrodite to guide her, she began…

In the same way as when she was with Zen Sanders, Andie wanted their relationship kept between the two of them, not to share it for the world to see on Valentine's Night Ghosts. Andie managed to quite spectacularly fail in her quest for secrecy before their investigation even began, as viewers witnessing her breathlessly moving aside Rada's hair to kiss her ear and neck as they hugged a few moments before could confirm.

"Welcome to my solo here in cell five. Oh my gosh, Andie Valentine thinks of everything! I was in this cell earlier on today and no chair. Yet when she places her fixed camera here, she leaves me this chair. I feel sure you've already worked this out witnessing me calling her 'Ands' and our familiarity with one another, Andie and I are girlfriends. I'll leave a comment for her when she edits. Thank you Ands, volim te!"

Realising it that would be impossible for her to edit out the 'kissing incident' from their video without affecting continuity, emotionally intelligent Rada decided she'd better explain all straight away, especially for the sake of Ands reputation with her viewers. She realised the most effective way would be 'innocently' sharing on-camera Andie is her girlfriend, She'd intentionally used Croatian, then it would seem to her followers they had history, and naturally Andie would fully understand what she'd said. In case you don't speak Croatian, when Rada said volim te, it means I love you. Rada fully understood if Andie didn't want to come-out to her followers, allowing several seconds gap, so she could easily edit it out and use only the statement she would make the next moment.

Rada declared "There is a spirit in here with me, already I sense him, soon we'll see if he talks to me!"

Having recorded her introduction and exonerated Andie, Rada turned off her hand-held camera, the in-situ fixed camera was yet to be turned on. Rada sat herself on the chair Andie did genuinely leave her, smoothing her long dress over her knees. Rada's phone camera acted as her mirror, applying clear lip-gloss and arranging her blonde hair out of the way over her shoulders. Andie insisted she must turn-off her phone, acting as instructed Rada did this and was ready for her solo!

*****

She'd strangely never before felt any desire sit all alone in the pitch dark in her own cellars; panning around the room with her flashlight, she took in her surroundings.

Rada turned on the fixed camera "This cell is small, okay I am not especially a tall chick at 176cm, but watch this, sitting I reach out and see how easily I touch the walls either side at once! The length of the cell is three metres, perhaps long enough for some kind of sleeping mattress, I hope at least the inmates they had this! High on the wall over there is the tiny window with those bars, I know for myself, little natural light enters in here during daytime. Odours in here I try to describe for you. It smells old! Is this making sense? Not damp, but kind of heavy with all the history hanging in the air. It is claustrophobic, never usually my issue, but I confess with the door closed like this, irrationally I feel scarily trapped!" Rada shifted the fixed camera, momentarily focussing on the closed door. "This and the other four cells down here were in use for about twenty years from 1840. I am trying vision what it must have been like down here when this building was new, before these rooms were cells; I wonder what these spaces were used for?" Meanwhile, thoroughly occupied with the nasty spirit residing in the creepy room, Andie Valentine's solo was uncovering the full horror of what the cellar space once was used for, but more of that in the next chapter.

Meanwhile, Rada continued her narrative into the fixed camera "Oh my days, the atmosphere is heavy in here! I wonder how many poor souls once occupying this same room in which I sit were ever getting acquitted, or was it finding yourself in one of these cells, meaning you would be going to jail proper or getting hung?"

She stared around herself wide eyed "Oh my gosh, I now hear a scratching noise from over by the cell door! I hope the camera picks up on the sound! There are never any rodents in these cellars or anywhere else within Kostović, properly I ensure this, regularly we are inspected to be sure and never they find any rodent. This scratching noise must be paranormal; this is way out cool for like my first ever solo!" Rada panned her flashlight around the room.

"I switch on my Spirit Box; it is believed that spirits may communicate directly with us through this device. Oh my gosh, this is so noisy! I watch Andie using this multiple times on Valentine's Night Ghosts, this is my first time in a confined space with the Spirit Box, it is freakily loud!" Rada tried adjusting the volume which made no practical difference "Ands, gets good results using the Spirit Box, let us see how I get on!"

Looking around the cell, Rada declared "I swear I feel the despair of previous occupants in this cell; like these four walls around me absorbed all their fear!" Rada sensed she needed to move things along.

After taking a sip of water from the bottle she'd brought along with her; she asked "Is there anyone in this room with me please? I would never dream of harming you and I come here with respect. Please do not be afraid of this ridiculously noisy device I hold in my hand, if you talk I will hear you, please communicate with me!"

She waited with bated breath to see if any spirits would talk to her "Nothing so far is coming through. This scary sounding device does not harm you I promise. I would love to know your story, please talk to me!"

Out of the blue a male voice could be heard on the Spirit Box saying "Girl!" Rada refers to herself as 'chick', being non-native English she enjoys the sound of the word; she also loves the sound of biscuit, daffodil and stevedore, of course she doesn't identify as any of those. Since turning twenty-one years old, the word she passionately hasn't identified with though is 'girl'. Ask Rada, she'll respond she's a hippie-chick vegan bar owner or put another way, Rada identifies as a businesswoman. Ask this question of Andie, she would doubtless describe Rada as some living goddess. Practically nothing causes the eternally chilled Rada to lose her cool, however, unless someone wishes to experience the fully unleashed wrath of one seriously vexed Croatian, better they never dare call her a girl!

Rada tersely responded to the Spirit Box "Thank you for that, but I am adult woman!" More gently she asked "Do you see me?" Through the indicative Spirit Box wave of deafening static, this same male voice admonished her "I see you wench, you shouldn't be here!" Somewhat taken aback at being told to leave, Rada stated "My name, it is Joy" and after a pause enquired "What is your name? Please tell me why I shouldn't be here"

Rada, knowing her name might confuse the spirit, opted to rename herself the literal meaning of her name - Joy.

"Joy?" The spirit repeated her name, an excited Rada declared "Oh my gosh, thank you lovely person! Yes, I am Joy, please can you share your name and tell me why I shouldn't be in here!" Several minutes passed by "Hung me!" Through the loud background static, Rada barely comprehended what he said, using intuition she worked it out "I am so sorry to be hearing this! Are you concerned I too will get myself hung because I sit in this same cell as you?" He admonished her again "You must leave here wench!"

In her head, Rada asked Aphrodite to guide her.

Rada asked "Please say my name again, to be sure you really talk to me, what is your name lovely person?" And after two minutes of hearing only static "Joy. Jake"

Rada felt an adrenaline rush washing over her, she was in direct communication with the spirit in her cellar and she knew his name! "Hello Jake! Please tell me who is the monarch?" He replied "Victoria" and asked "Frenchie?" Not understanding the question, she replied "What does Frenchie mean Jake?" Quite ironic, as we'll discover later. Rada got nothing but static coming from her Spirit Box. Turning it off for a moment, she briefly switched on her phone and searched for Frenchie.

Rada smiled to herself and turned the Spirit Box on "Jake, I am not Frenchie. I come from the place far from France!" She heard static and nothing else "Are you there Jake? If you used up all your energy talking with me, please can you make a noise in this cell to let me know you are still here" Rada turned off the Spirit Box to listen.

"Did you here that? A tapping noise from cell door! Oh, please let microphone on the camera be picking up this; is that you Jake? Please tap twice if that is you" Two of the faintest of taps. "Oh gosh, this is too cool! Thank you! Jake, please may I ask you the few more questions? If yes tap twice, if not tap only once. Two faint tapping noises again!"

"I follow my intuition asking questions, Ands swears I am psychic, let us test if truly I am as she claims! Right here goes. Jake, I feel you were stealing food, is this what gets you in trouble?" Two barely audible taps "Please let this be heard on the camera! Thank you for tapping, Jake you have the family, yes?" Two taps "And you steal to feed them?" Two even fainter taps "Thank you lovely! And I feel like I bother you enough now. I sense you are tired from this. I am leaving you to rest. Thank you so much for communicating with me tonight, Jake!" Tears welled up in Rada's eyes. Not wanting to ruin her eye make-up, she softly dabbed at them with a tissue. She succeeded in not actually crying and her eye make-up survived intact.

*****

Taking a few minutes out to compose herself; Rada went back on-camera to record her outro, summing up how she'd felt about her investigation "I do not know if this was beginner's luck, but this exceed everything I dream of. I talked to Jake, a man getting hung for trying to feed his family. I try not judge those times; but for sure this is awful, and what about his poor family! I wonder what became of them? We know the era in which Jake lived, that of Queen Victoria, my intuition says around 1850? We never know this for sure obviously, the court records from those days will all be long lost. I wonder how Andie Valentine is getting on with her solo investigation of the creepy room? Let's go there now to find out!"

Despite the rollercoaster of emotions she'd experienced, Rada had the presence of mind to remember that her solo would be getting shown first and link to Andie's solo in her outro.

3

Andie Valentine wasn't too disappointed by her actions. Rada smelled divine and was gorgeous, she felt it would be too impolite not to kiss her! Practically speaking, she wondered how she could edit it out of their video without compromising the continuity.

And then she heard Rada's introduction to her solo...

After she'd ostensibly left to walk away to her own solo, ensuring Rada felt okay in there all alone, Andie doubled back and stood outside the door of cell five for a couple of minutes after Rada had entered. She could hear Rada speaking on-camera, beginning with her introduction.

'What a fricking goddess of a woman!' Andie thought, as Rada immediately informed Andie's followers, they'd surely already worked out they are girlfriends and that she loves Andie. Naturally she understood everything behind why Rada declared this and used Croatian. Andie Valentine wanted to burst straight into cell five, and in all likelihood French kiss Rada. On-camera. Oops!

Realising Rada would be more than capable on her own, Andie left the door outside of cell five to make her way off to her own solo.

She smiled to herself at her wish to keep their loved-up status between the two of them never standing a chance. Yeah, she already kissed Rada on-camera, but even if she hadn't, she knew when they investigated together later there was no way she could pretend Rada was only the owner of the bar she got called in to investigate. How she gazed at Rada would immediately give away everything! They agreed to rendezvous in Rada's office after their solos. She had a hunch it might be some time later before they made their way to investigate The Coach and Horses Function Suite together.

*****

Andie Valentine began her walk down the narrow annex leading towards the infamous creepy room. Right 'time to focus' she told herself, she knew she would need to be on her A-Game for what lay ahead of her. She turned on her hand-held camera, with no intention of editing Rada's intro to remove any content and knowing her solo would be shown straight after hers, she began her introduction.

"My girlfriend Rada, the owner of Kostović, refers to this location I'm off to investigate as 'That creepy room with the nasty spirit!' Earlier as I set up my fixed camera in the room, too well I understand what she means; I the need to warn you before you watch, my solo tonight could well be the most extreme ever shown on Valentine's Night Ghosts!"

Halfway down the annex corridor she stopped "I want to show you this on the wall. In case my camera's night-time vision doesn't pick this up, I'll also pan my flashlight to illuminate it better for you. See those 'ghost stairs' there outlined in the wall? Rada told me these were directly under the original bar, back when this was The Coach and Horses. I'm feeling awful energy emanating from these 'ghost stairs' which makes me wonder, were they only used for bringing beer up to the bar, or have they a more malevolent past?" Andie gave her trademark 'mysterious stare' into her camera.

"Okay, here goes nothing! I'm now entering 'That creepy room with the nasty spirit!' As you see it's a large room. Excuse me one moment, I'll go silent while I assess what we're dealing with here! I'll switch the fixed camera on and leave this one running as I explore. Talk to you soon to let you know what I know!"

She walked across to the wardrobe like alcove, stepping into the space, she felt a menacing presence immediately. Clearly this space was of some significance to this entity!

Opting to remain in the space, she reached out to see if she could get anything psychic coming back from this spirit. "There's a shadow figure standing right in front of

103

me, he's attempting to block me from leaving this odd little alcove! I hope this shows up on-camera" it did…

The fixed camera showed Andie standing in the alcove, a faint misty dark cloud s directly in front of her. "Hmm, I need to waking meditate to get a sense of what went on down here! Regular viewers you'll know what I'm talking about my, if you're new here, this meditation helps me to 'vision' past events"

*****

In her head Andie Valentine heard Zen Sanders telling her "Trust me darling, this creature is not any demon. Andie, he's a human spirit. You've so freaking got this darling! Sailors!" Although she reasoned it was unlikely her recent ex-boyfriend Zen Sanders, astral travelled from London to Liverpool to help her in Kostović, she couldn't quite rule this out. If he sensed she was in danger, who's to say he wasn't there to help her? They worked closely together for those ten months, having each other's backs through Zen Sanders's demonic cases. Andie put hearing his encouraging voice in her head down to something akin to muscle memory.

Andie was undisputedly an expert on the paranormal, during four years of experience there's little in the way of spooky she hasn't met. Exorcising of demons or extreme negative entities however was not within her own area of expertise. Ghosts she could exorcise, demons not.

Due to his ten years of experience, Zen Sanders possessed a degree with first class honours in kicking the ass of any demon and nasty spirit! Had they been investigating in the cellar, Andie's role would have been supporting Zen, while he dealt with the negative entity, which she would have realised by adding her personal energy to his. Or in other words, holding Zen's hand for protection while he did his thing!

To avoid their viewers thinking it's a good idea to copy Zen, to end up in a right royal pickle as a demon devours their immortal soul, they never showed his exorcisms in full on-camera. Andie's ghost exorcisms were also heavily edited on film, for the same reason.

Her erstwhile partner had once informed her "Andie, you think you're far too nice to kick the ass of demons or shitty spirits. Trust me on this Andie, given the right motivation, you freaking could and would!"

Feeling out of her depth with the prospect of exorcising demonic spirits was obviously the reason she'd suggested to Rada in her car she might be able to contain the nasty but couldn't exorcise him all by herself or in other words, without Zen Sanders to do it for her!

Andie pondered what hearing Zen speaking in her head all meant, she deduced there must be a message for her in there somewhere.

*****

'Sailors!' what could this actually mean? Feeling a surge of energy, Andie saw everything through her sixth sense. The entire awful history loomed crystal clear!

She began narrating a stream-of-consciousness dialogue directly into her fixed camera "Almost immediately The Coach and Horses opened its doors for business a truly evil trade was going on in this cellar, it was used for the forced subscription of sailors into the navy! Men already merchant sailors and those who weren't seafarers, but yet young and able bodied, upon entering The Coach and Horses seeking ale, found themselves befriended by this lovely maiden. As the alcohol freely flowed, the maiden slipped a dose of laudanum into his beer. Now suitably disorientated, she led him by the hand behind the bar and down the steps back along the passage and into this very room, This is where her employer stood waiting for him in that alcove. In his befuddled state and now thinking he would be getting his way with the fine maiden, he let his guard down. He would never hear the thug creeping up behind him. Coshed hard on the head with a blackjack, instantly the man was rendered unconscious. Should he awaken later, many didn't, victims of too high dosage of laudanum or over heavy-handed coshing, the dead were easily disposed of into the Mersey; the unfortunate man would soon discover himself aboard a navy ship far out at sea, forced to work or get thrown overboard! The evil creature supplying these unwilling sailors got well paid for delivering them"

The sound of footsteps shuffling all around Andie on the dirt floor, she ignored them, and feeling more energised than she could ever recall, continued her narrative.

"This evil creature finally met his match when this giant of a man got befriended by the lovely maiden in the bar. Thinking him sufficiently drugged on laudanum, down she brought him into the arms of her employer, however, this bear of a man was discovered to be nowhere near as helpless as they'd imagined! Shrugging off the effects of ingesting enough laudanum to render several cart horses unconscious, he fought back, snatching the blackjack off the thug, he made good use of it, promptly killing him by bludgeoning him multiple times about the head! Not desiring to suffer the same fate as her recently deceased employer, the fair maiden pleaded with him to allow her to take her leave of his company, quoting 'Get thee to a nunnery!' he allowed the maiden to go. This giant man passed untroubled by anyone through the crowded bar, walking out of the door never to be seen again in town. Later that same day, the fully complicit landlord of The Coach and Horses disappeared. He too was never seen again in town" These words tumbled out of her one after the other. Our narrator breathed, becoming all too aware of the present day...and the truth.

Andie understood this disgusting thing had physically affected Rada by giving her migraine headaches! Still within her waking mediation, full of dawning horror, she intuited he intended destroying Rada's beauty, marking her deeply across her entire face with his signature three scratches, then she would always remember him!

Andie immediately felt white hot with rage and resolved there and then she'd instantly do what Zen Sanders would if he were there! Exorcize this shitty entity from off the face of the planet, or as Zen would put it, she'd 'Kick his freaking ass straight to hell!' before he had any chance of harming her lovely Rada!!!

The yelling Andie Valentine proclaimed "You've no right to exist on this earth! You will leave this place! Leave this building this very moment! Your power over anyone or anything is over! Begone from here never to return!!!" The creature attempted to resist, before the authority of Andie Valentine's commands he was completely helpless; she screamed out at the top of her lungs the final part of her exorcism "Tremble before the irresistible power of the Goddess Freyja, and in her name I command you begone and to never return!!!"

The evil spirit was instantly banished. Rada was safe and Andie wondered how the heck she'd just did that! Picking up her discarded hand-held camera from off the floor, she turned it back on and recorded the outro.

"Rada's 'Creepy room with the nasty spirit!' Is free of the nasty spirit! It feels above anything else peaceful in here. For our next investigation Rada and I will join forces, as we head to The Coach and Horses Function Suite, we'll discover if court is still in session and what's causing the poltergeist type activity"

As she'd instructed Rada earlier, without fail on any case Andie diligently switches off her phone. This isn't only for not getting disturbed; she doesn't want its emissions compromising the integrity of her equipment's responses.

Impossibly her phone now pinged, heralding the arrival of a new text message 'Astral darling. Freaking ass-kicker! Proud. Knew you could. Twin-Flames two halves of same soul. She's yours. Blessed be x' it read.

Andie was fully aware of who'd sent her this impossible text message. Although no longer listed as a contact, his number was indelibly printed in her subconscious.

4

Andie carried the two fixed cameras with her when she left the cellars on her way for their rendezvous in Rada's office. She left them outside the cellar door; she'd pick them up again as they passed by on their way upstairs to their next investigation.

Their cellar solos ended within ten minutes of one other, Rada's before hers. Entering in the security code for the door, she found her office illuminated by the soft glow of candlelight and the sensual fragrance of jasmine incense filling the air. She gazed at Rada reclining full length on the Chesterfield, wearing her gift from the goddess smile, mystery perfume and nothing else.

With the impossible text message in her thoughts, softly she said "Volim te Rada" For the first time in her twenty-three years she understood what genuine love feels like.

Equally unfettered by now with attire, she joined Rada on the Chesterfield. Rada breathlessly replied "I always love you Ands, throughout so many lives!" Instantly she fully comprehended Twin-Flames. Equally breathlessly Andie responded "I feel you Rada, I've always known your soul. Yes, us twin flames within our transcending love!" Rada's gift from the goddess smile was especially radiant. By the romance of candlelight, Andie and Rada gazed into one another's windows of the soul,. Remembering.

*****

Later on that night they left Rada's office. The Coach and Horses Function Suite could wait no more, and their first investigation together was officially underway.

They allowed the safety and comfort of leaving on all the lights while they walked up the stairs and Andie set up the fixed cameras. Unlike in the cellar, each room had its own light switches, oh the decadence!

She placed one camera panning from the stage across the dancefloor and covering all the room. The other camera monitored the cushion on the 'haunted chair' hoping it would it obligingly do its thing on-camera.

"Welcome to The Coach and Horses Function Suite for part two of our investigation into the spirits at Kostović. Owner Rada Kostović is alongside me ready for anything this room throws at us!" She panned her hand-held onto her and Rada waved to their viewers "I do mean literally throws at us! Taking my usual daylight walk-through to familiarize myself with where I'll later be wandering around in the dark, Rada and I experienced something paranormal! As we were about to exit out of that door" She panned onto the exit "A loud crashing noise came from behind us, we did an abrupt about-turn, running back to investigate! Rada, please share the rest of the story"

"Oh my gosh Ands! We ran straight to where the noise seemed to come, beyond the bar. Arriving we find a beer bottle laid on the floor, and still it rolls a little. I pick up this bottle and I place it back on the shelf it came from. We look at each other, we know it could not have fallen by itself! I am not feeling so scared, this kind of thing, it is happening all the time in Kostović!"

Andie Valentine said "Let's do this Rada; time to switch those lights off and start on our second investigation in Kostović Where we'll perhaps meet a poltergeist, or is it another entity causing mischief? We'll fully investigate to see if court is still in session as well"

Rada continued with the introduction "Andie and I have our hand-held cameras, plus there are two fixed cameras; one panning the room for anything we don't catch with our own eyes. The other camera sits upon this table over here" They walked across the room "The cushion on this chair fixed camera two is focussed on is believed to press down alike someone unseen sits there! We have some equipment with us; let's move over to the bar before we begin properly exploring this floor. I have the Spirit Box; I achieve much success with this on my solo earlier. I now power it up and we can see if anyone or anything would like to say hello!" She added "It is said the spirits, they talk to us through this equipment, this ludicrously noisy device I hold in my hand"

Rada called out "Hello, I am asking if there is anyone in here who would like to talk to us. I am called Joy, this is my friend Andie" Rada pointed with the psychedelic little finger of her right hand at Andie, who raised one eyebrow and grinned when Rada called herself Joy "We mean you no harm or disrespect, we love if you would talk with us and share your story"

They waited, listening intently, making sure they didn't miss anything "Joy!" Came over the Spirit Box after a minute or so; Rada knew who this was "Jake, I thank you for also coming up here to talk with me! Do you know if any other spirits are in this room Jake?" After a moment Jake announced "He is gone!" Andie said "I know Jake, you're free of him!" Jake responded "Joy?" Glancing at one another, Rada resumed asking the questions "I am here Jake! Do you not see me?" After a few minutes of hearing just static feedback "I can see you Joy!" Andie whispered to "Jake would have been tried in this room; it's likely not his fav place to revisit as a spirit! He really must want to talk further with you Rada!"

"Jake, I know how you must feel about room. Thank you so much for following me up here from the cellar" Rada stated "Do you know if other spirits are in the room?" Instantly he said "Fairest wench!" Rada looked seriously uncomfortable with where this was all heading! Andie squeezed her hand, encouraging her to continue on "Are there any other spirits in here?" Jake's response to this "I will lay with you my fairest wench!" Rada immediately turned off the Spirit Box and stated into Andie's camera "Jake, I stop talking with you because I do not like what you say! I know you are coming from another time but if we are to talk again, you must be respecting me, please do not ever be saying those things!"

Andie added into Rada's camera "Joy is not some serving wench bringing you your ale Jake. She is Lady Joy coming from a faraway land!" Rada covered up her face with her hands, attempting and failing to disguise her laughter. Although Rada's had never worked in her own bar pulling pints, she effectively *was* a serving wench bringing ale to all her customers! They left the cameras rolling but paused their investigation, allowing Rada time to stop laughing. "Très magnifique, merci Ands. Je t'aime!" Rada finally declared, when able to talk again. It didn't register with habitually observant Andie that her Croatian girlfriend spoke to her in perfectly enunciated French expressing how she loved her for making her laugh.

With calmness once more reigning, they resumed.

114

They could hear persistent tapping on the entrance door, intuitively Rada turned the Spirit Box back on "Lady Joy!" Rada glanced briefly at Andie, hoping that she wouldn't start laughing again and replied "I am here" Three minutes of static followed, until faintly "Respect you" Followed in one minute by "Lady Joy" Which could now barely be heard. "Thank you Jake, I am most happy you say this to me. I am sensing you need to rest now. Please be resting" No other communications came through the Spirit Box from Jake that night, however their investigation in the function suite was only just getting started!

*****

"Did you hear that?!" This came from Rada. Andie asked "Tell me what you heard babes and let's see if this is what I'm sure I did" Rada looked into Andie's camera "Like the sound of a judge's hammer slamming down, What you call it Ands, that thing he is banging?" She smiled "Yeah, that's what I heard too! It's called a gavel Rada. I'm hoping one of our cameras in here picked this noise up!" Her own hand-held camera had.

They walked across the room to the small stage, formally the location where the judge would once have sat. "Ooh it is cold here Ands, watch this, here it feel like heatwave we have in England at the moment, here for sure I need a cardigan!" Rada illustrated her point by initially standing up on the stage, stepping off it and then back on.

"Babe try the Spirit Box on the stage" Andie suggested.

Rada turned on the Spirit Box, having already decided after the Jake incident authenticity was the way forward, she introduced them "This is Andie, I am called Rada, we would love to talk with you!"

Immediately a loud scream cut through the static "Who screamed then?" Andie asked. The distinctive sound of a gavel banging once more, this time heard over the Spirit Box. Andie postulated "I think we're hearing the residual sounds from a trail that took place like two hundred years ago Rada!" She replied "Oh my gosh Andie!"

Another piercing scream came over the Spirit Box. Rada turned it off; clearly Andie wanted to say something.

"There is a theory about time and residual noises" Andie stated. "Please be sharing this theory!" Rada responded. She said "I know this is going to sound weird, however, the theory goes when we hear noises they're not always a haunting! They're 'stone tape memory' sounds. By stone tape memory, I mean the walls or objects surrounding experiences of strong emotions such as grief or trauma, absorb these events, If paranormal investigators like us come along Rada, those past events can be heard over our equipment!"

"Babes, I think about this as you talk, what you say makes perfect sense. Yet I form another theory!" Rada declared. Andie literally couldn't have looked more in love with the woman if she'd tried. She said "Babes, please share your theory; I'm fascinated to hear what you think!"

Wearing her gift from the goddess smile on her face, Rada said "I am thinking Ands, if we may hear sounds from the long past, alike we listen to a download. Is it possible this is through type of, oh what is the name? Portal! I should know this word working in Bold Street! I am wondering if this is portal, and it works both ways. Those voices and noises we hear are not, as you say, because of stone tape memory, perhaps they too hear us speaking, thinking of course they are hearing ghosts! Oh my gosh Andie, if this is true, all the screams we hear on our Spirit Box are from people from the past freaking out about the 'ghosts' they are hearing! Which are really us!" Rada gazed expectantly at Andie, awaiting her reaction.

Andie replied "What a concept Rada! I can't disagree with any of your theory. Pondering all the implications of this is frankly incredible! Do some locations become known as haunted because there's a history of voices being heard, yet are these voices paranormal investigators calling out to spirits through a portal? The people of the past, hearing these voices, as you've suggest Rada, mean wherever the future guys are investigating has a reputation for being hunted, but is it really haunted at all? Oh my gosh! As you would say. Stone tape memory theory does explain some genuine residual sound, however what you're suggesting in your theory could also explain so much Rada!" Andie kissed her, long past caring if this was on-camera.

A soft metallic banging noise, seemingly originating from the kitchenette. As we know, Andie hadn't entered this room during her daytime tour, intentionally leaving it for later exploration during her investigation .

They walked over to the kitchen, shining their flashlights to get a sense of what in that room might have caused the noise. Andie observed catering-style metal surfaces, a six-ring gas hob, two ovens and a 'dumb waiter' in the corner, presumably linked to the larger downstairs main kitchen to bring ingredients up when this kitchenette was in use. Non-slip green tiles covered the floor. Pans hung on the wall above the stove ready for use, the soft metallic noise they heard must have been a pan being gently struck like a gong!

Rada proclaimed "Andie there is something here with us in this room, I feel this without doubt, do you feel it too?" Andie responded "Yeah Rada. I've got a SLS camera app on my tablet" She dug out her tablet from backpack and passed it over to Rada "Open it Rada, let's see if anything shows up" Rada professionally explained "The SLS app marks out spirits and the living alike as these sort of stick persons on the screen"

Andie was seriously impressed by Rada Kostović, when the woman said she'd watched her channel right from day one she wasn't exaggerating! She couldn't fault her techie knowledge and fully appreciated her easy way of explaining their investigation equipment and what it did for the benefit of their viewers.

Zen Sanders hadn't been too conscious of viewers, to him investigating was all about the excitement of kicking the ass of anything remotely demonic! Thinking to offer any explanation about their equipment or what it was being used for, quite literally never crossed the man's mind. He left all that to Andie.

Andie said "I mentioned earlier on, in my introduction, the history of poltergeist type activity on this floor and in the main bar downstairs. I now need to explain before we investigate, not every poltergeist I encounter is evil, far from it! They're mischievous and do enjoy creating their 'floor-show' but would never intentionally hurt humans. I think this is that type of poltergeist we're dealing with here in Kostović. Rada, it doesn't feel threatening to me, what do you sense?" She replied "Not threatening at all Ands, there are glasses falling onto the wooden floor and never they break; my customers and staff, they are getting touched on elbow or shoulder; and then there are noises, like this making us investigate this kitchen. Oui, I agree entirely with you, this spirit for sure feels mischievous but like totally cool, not scary or nasty"

Rada turned on their SLS app "Andie, there is the figure stood on kitchen surface directly in front of us!" Rada had already zoomed her camera in closely onto the tablet, so their viewers could see exactly what she saw "It seems like the figure is dancing Ands!" She excitedly observed, then "Oh, then he is gone!" She addressed her girlfriend "Andie, you have a thermal imaging app, I see you use it before. I turn off SLS and seek app. Oh, I find it! Thermal imaging, it shows heat signatures, anything paranormal most usually emits a cold energy, we should be able to see this entity as a blue cold spot if still he is here"

Andie Valentine was becoming in awe of Rada's ability to put across what their investigations equipment did in one easily understandable sentence. Andie appreciated how especially impressive this was considering Rada wasn't even talking in her first language! Mind you, neither was she…

"You need to see this!" Rada had focussed her camera in again onto the tablet "Look, there next to the stove Ands, there is the handprint!" Andie couldn't look over Rada's shoulder, she's way taller than her, therefore she placed her arm around her waist "I see what you mean Rada, a clear hand showing up as a cold spot on the metal surface. Not sure there's any point in trying the Spirit Box, if this genuinely is a poltergeist he's more than likely unable to communicate"

As the watched one of the oven doors fell open!

"Andie, this is wonderful!! I want to try talking with him. I am called Rada, you already know me I think, I want to tell you I am okay with you being in this building. You must never hurt anyone, but I feel sure you would not be doing this. Stay around if you behave yourself, please be giving me some sign you understand me!"

The same soft metallic sound initially drawing them into the kitchen could be heard, and a large frying pan gently rocked back and forth.

"Ands, I talk to him and I ask him to respond if he hears me and understands; immediately the pan it gets struck, this is him replying, yes?" She answered "Too much of a coincidence if it wasn't him responding. Communicate more Rada, and let's see if anything else happens!"

121

"Thank you for responding! Ands, for sure this spirit, he does not want to hurt us but he enjoys the attention, yes?" Andie responded "I agree Rada, although he's here in this kitchenette and directly in front of us, not in any sense does he feel threatening! Please try talking more babes"

Rada loved this! She asked "Do you know me? There is a cold signature on wall above gas hob, look Ands! Is this you making yourself seen a way of saying yes? Please do move if you understand me" The thermal image on the app slowly faded away. Andie said "I think you just got your answer Rada!" Andie smiled at her and got blessed with a delighted gift from the goddess smile "Although easily I could stay in here for the rest of night, I wonder should next go back into the function room Ands?" She agreed "Yeah Rada, we still need to investigate that chair with the moving cushion, let's go do this now"

*****

They turned off their cameras for a few moments as both investigators needed a comfort break. While they made their way back upstairs to resume with their investigation "Andie, you are cool I tell viewers about the equipment and I take lead sometimes?" Rada asked, she responded "It's awesome, gorgeous! You've watched how it usually works, even when Zen was alongside me, I'm always the one needing to describe

122

every item of kit for every single episode; and basically I directed where the investigation went next. I enjoy this investigation all the more because you're so mega capable and confident talking on-camera. I'm relaxed alongside you precisely because I don't need to think of everything!" Rada sighed out loud in relief "I confess I am used to decision making, owning Kostović since twenty-four years old. Most gratifying you saying it's all cool for me to occasionally take the lead. I did not want to seem to your viewers like I am taking over Valentine's Night Ghosts!" Andie giggled "I'm positive you'd never comes across like that Rada! Please keep on doing what you've done so far and all is cool!"

Rada winked "You are sure we do not have the time for 'us' before we must continue? Aphrodite would approve!" They turned their hand-held cameras back on.

Andie began "Since we arrived in the function suite for the second part of our investigation, fixed camera two has been filming this 'haunted chair'! We'll go through all the footage later to see if anything has shown up. Which I'll insert right here!" Nothing showed up. Andie continued explaining "What I thought we might do Rada, is invite the spirit enjoying sitting in this chair to make themselves known through some direct interaction. As the owner of Kostović, it seems more fitting if it's you who makes the invitation Rada"

They hadn't discussed this beforehand, nevertheless Rada immediately understood "Hi, please join us for a drink!" The women sat themselves down at the table, obviously leaving the 'haunted chair' vacant "We leave your chair free for you, please come and enjoy a drink with us!"

They waited, Andie's hand-held camera focussed closely in on the seat cushion "Is it my imagination Rada or did that cushion move ever so slightly?" Rada put her hand on the cushion "Ooh, it is freezing cold Ands! Thank you, it is good to enjoy a drink with you! We need to leave in a moment, however, please stay for as long as you please and enjoy another drink. Perhaps we sit with you another time and have a drink. Thank you lovely!"

*****

Taking her cue from Rada, Andie recorded her outro into fixed camera two "Part two draws to a close Rada. The Coach and Horses Function Suite did not disappoint! You spoke with Jake, a spirit you already know from your solo cellar lockdown. Jake fancies you Rada, yet in all honestly who wouldn't fancy you?" Rada surprisingly blushed. The woman 'does' bashful and shy? Who would have thought?!

To conclude, Andie summed up "We heard the court still in session, and those disembodied screams. In the kitchen we met with a mischievous poltergeist and lastly enjoyed a drink with a ghost!"

A still blushing Rada said "Next we investigate the Main Bar, back where we began tonight. Andie Valentine tries out cool new equipment she's never used before! See you there in one moment"

5

It was already after six o'clock when they set-up camp in the Main Bar. They needed to now get their skates on and conclude their investigation before Kostović opened for business on Tuesday morning.

Off-camera Andie asked "Who opens up in the morning, is it you Rada?" She shook her head "Chef Anton starts before any of us with his kitchen prep. And Chef Anton arrives at 8pm, we have not so long Ands! Tomorrow, oh I mean today, I take the day off, please come upstairs to spend the day with me Andie. Claudia does not require her parking space until Thursday"

Andie Valentine's smile was nearly as radiant as Rada's gift from the goddess one "Sounds like too good an offer for me to refuse Rada!" They giggled.

"Andie Valentine will try the Estes Method in my Main Bar! She has wanted to try this for a while but never felt comfortable. Andie wears noise cancelling headphones, into which is plugged the Spirit Box. She has a blindfold so she is not influenced by me or anything else. Let's test. Are you able to hear me Ands?" She didn't respond, any and all extraneous noises drowned in the static emanating from the Spirit Box.

"My role is to be asking the spirits questions, and Andie should hear their replies and tell us what they say"

Rada only subscribed to Valentine's Night Ghosts and no other paranormal channels. She'd never actually heard of The Estes Method. Andie explained all as they made their way downstairs and set up just the one fixed camera on the bar. Rada carried her hand-held camera, which she used to film herself The fixed camera covered Andie sat on a bar stool in front of it.. Rada naturally got The Estes Method straight away, easily and intuitively understanding the type of questions she need to ask to get responses.

Rada "Hello I am called Rada. My friend Andie will hear if you talk and tell me what you say"

Andie "Cheers! *This is a male voice*"

Rada "Cheers to you. Are you drinking in the bar?"

Andie Hi! *Same male voice*"

Rada "Hi! What year is it please?"

Andie "I am here"

Rada "I know you are. Please talk to my friend, tell her what the year is"

Andie "Double oh seven. *I hear laughter Rada*"

Rada "Do you mean it is 2007?"

Andie "Martini not stirred! *I hear laughter again*"

Rada "How old are you?

Andie "I died. Accent!"

Rada "Most sorry to be hearing this. I am Croatian, that is my accent. How did you die?"

Andie "Fell. Head. Died"

Rada "In here, you died in bar?"

Andie *"He doesn't want to say anything else, I sense he died in this bar not so long before you took over"*

Rada "Thank you for talking lovely person! Please, are there any other of the spirits wanting to communicate with us. This is a chance to tell your story. Me friend, she can hear you and tells me what you say"

Andie *"Really deep male voice saying angel. I could just about make out this word"*

Rada "Sir, why do you say angel?"

Andie "I"

Rada "Do you mean eye or I"

Andie "Justice, Eye for Eye"

Rada "Help me to understand Sir"

Andie "Angel. Evil. Farewell!"

Rada "Please do not go Sir, I want to understand!"

Andie "Angel"

Rada "You are an angel or Angel is your name?"

Andie "I am all"

Rada "Please explain what you mean, Have you been drinking in this pub"

Andie " Aye, I drank here. I am Angel. Fare thee well purest of fair maidens!"

Rada "Thank you for talking Sir"

No other spirits communicated after this. And with that their investigation of Kostović concluded.

Andie Valentine filmed her outro "What a night this has been at Kostović! It certainly didn't disappoint. Rada, my love and thanks for inviting me along to investigate your bar It's seven o'clock, soon Kostović opens for business. Rada, it's about time we went home!"

Rada nodded in the affirmative "Thank you for watching our investigation, maybe I see you again, stranger things happen. I wish you love, peace and goodest vibes!" She made a peace sign and blew a kiss into the camera.

A CITY WITH NO NAME
Steel and concrete
Stark and bleak
PART FOUR

1

They exited Rada's lift into her studio and living space. Rada kicked off her shoes "I would be barefooted always if I could Ands, do you enjoy barefooted?" Andie smiled "In my home I never wear any shoes" Rada asked "Andie, please dance with me!" Andie thought she was getting used to Rada's surrealist mind, still she managed to say the unexpected. Cool as anything, Andie replied "Waltz?" They waltzed around the studio with Andie leading.

Rada talked as they waltzed; her lovely gentle voice was like the softest lullaby to Andie "I am delighted we leave before Chef Anton arrives. Usually he is divine Ands but obsesses about his routine getting disrupted. If for any reason this happens, we keep out of the way from Chef Anton until he calms down! I am lucky to employ him in Kostović; he loves Liverpool and adores the freedom; I let him to run the kitchen his way. Formerly he worked at a top vegan eatery in London, he has been with me from firstly I open my doors, much of the success of Kostović is surely all about Chef Anton! Always I ensure he feels happy within his kitchen. I am ordering any ingredients he requires immediately he asks of me. He is loyal to me. So talented. Claudia Augello, who you already meet Ands, and Chef Anton are the only two members of my staff to be with me since day one"

They stopped waltzing and made their way through to the kitchen, Rada went into her full barista mode, Andie asked "If you had yet to open Rada, how the heck did you manage to recruit both Chef Anton and lovely Claudia?" Rada explained "This man walks into what is basically a construction site not too long after I begin renovations, he asks me if the owner is around. I inform him I am she! We talk for the while; he leaves me CV. Upon reading this, immediately I ask for another meeting! He agrees to help with kitchen design how he want it; the rest is the history"

Andie declared "Wow! Did you ever find out why he'd decided to stroll into basically this building site?" Rada laughed "I did babes! Already I place a sign in window saying vegan bar and restaurant open soon. Chef Anton, he spends a few days in Liverpool, regularly he visits to see soccer team he supports. He adores Bold Street, and upon seeing my sign, and being a vegan chef, he cannot resist entering and asking. I allow him time off to see his soccer team Liverpool, whenever this is possible. Oh my gosh! I am in love with his food, literally like best vegan cuisine I ever tasted and in my own restaurant! Like too cool, yes?" Andie replied "For sure Rada. I'm not vegan but I'd love to try Chef Anton's food!" Rada's enigmatic smile would have put Mona Lisa to shame "Yet" was all she softly said.

Exhausted and tired Andie hadn't the faintest idea what 'Yet' meant, so went instead with asking "Did Claudia also walk into your building site Rada?" Rada explained their history "Before Kostović I worked with Samantha-Jayne or Sammy-Jayne as Claudia calls her. SJ she was to me. SJ once she was my girlfriend. Subjectively babes, SJ was the prettier woman out of us two by far. After I leave where we work, to start my Kostović project, SJ and I drift apart as couple, yet stay closest friends. SJ informs me her new girlfriend seeks bar work. Of course I trust in SJ and that she would never suggest her girlfriend for a job if she didn't believe her most capable. Claudia, she arrives at Kostović for her interview, which by now resembles a bar instead of a demolition site. I take on Claudia there and then!"

Changing the subject entirely, as was her way, handing Andie her coffee, Rada said "I want you to feel as if my home is also your home" She sat opposite Andie at her kitchen table, reaching across to hold her hand. Rada now stated "After the coffee I have shower. I am up all night and I feel tired. I go to bed. You are free to do whatever you are wishing of course Andie, yet I would love if you did as me, and we cuddle up sleeping for several hours" Andie's tired smile said it all "Sounds perfect babes"

"Aphrodite, I ask you to protect Andie Valentine and me as we sleep. We thank you!" Rada proclaimed. In less than five minutes both women were sound asleep.

*****

Andie Valentine woke up first, at five in the afternoon. When she was able to confirm what she'd thought in her pondering a few days before. Waking up seeing Rada before anything else *did* make her feel very blessed!

Andie adored the minimalism of Rada's bedroom, fitting within her own design aesthetic perfectly. A comfortable mattress sat on the floor with no bedframe, one stripped pine wardrobe with a matching chest of drawers, and this was all Rada's substantial bedroom contained. Multiple large white candles placed on the floor around the room, hidden wall lights but no other lighting. Three windows overlooked Bold Street.

She felt Rada stretching out beside her waking up. Andie said "Hello!" The sleepy Rada responded "Hello Miss Valentine! On my days, I adore you A-Natural, une vraie beauté!!!" They arose from bed a full twenty-four hours after Andie's arrival in Liverpool the previous day at six pm.

Rada suggested "I order us vegan pizzas if you are okay with this? It is usual I cook but I want precious time with you instead!" Rada kissed her "Yes Rada, pizza is all cool by me and I've never tried a vegan pizza" Andie replied.

Over pizza, Andie asked "Rada, you mentioned a career before Kostović. What did you do?"

She grinned, not with her familiar gift from the goddess smile, altogether more mischievous "Try to guess!"

Andie smiled "When we talked in Artemis the Beetle, I remember you mentioned moving to Liverpool for Uni, to study something along the lines of ecology or climate. Were you and SJ some kind of environmental scientists?"

Rada giggled "I give you the clue Andie, I switched Uni courses over almost immediately. I qualified in another career. Two more guesses, then I tell all"

Andie studied Rada's gorgeous face and looked into her striking pale blue eyes "I've got it! Did you work with SJ in the beauty industry? I mean you claim she's prettier than you Rada. To borrow your expression, subjectively you're the loveliest hippie-chick I've ever seen! SJ's going to have people falling at her feet in worship wherever she goes if she's genuinely prettier than you babes!"

"SJ sort of does get something alike that happening to be honest, total strangers are always asking her out. By the way, you are not even warm yet Andie!" Tears from too much laughing rolled down Rada's cheeks "Okay, just one more guess!"

"I've got it, you were alternative therapists!"

Between giggles, Rada managed to say "SJ and I worked at a High School not too far from here. SJ still does. She teaches maths and my subject was French"

As we established earlier, Andie Valentine doesn't really do startled, at this news her mouth fell open in surprise! "You're a qualified French teacher Rada?!"

"Oui! I know I massacre English. French though I find so easy from the early age. I think of English like my fourth language after Croatian, French and Russian. If I really concentrate I can speak better English, look I show you!" Rada stood up "Hello and welcome to another episode of Valentine's Night Ghosts, if you're new here, Hi, I'm most sexy Andie Valentine" Rada perfectly mimicked Andie's rather posh English accent, without any trace of her own. "I get by in English, I do not feel a need to be perfect. Yet if I concentrate and copy English person's way of talking, I pass as native English. My Liverpool accent I am proud of extremely Andie. I know I tell you this already, I am in love with this city!"

"I meet my SJ at teacher training; we admit within few days of meeting we fancy each other. Soon we go out and we are the couple until I become obsessed with Kostović, and then we go our separate ways"

Andie asked "Have you only dated girls and women?"

Rada grinned "Nope! Oh my gosh, should I even tell you this Andie? Okay, no secrets, here goes. Chef Anton and me had this crazy thing after Kostović opens. Before my apartment is made I live with him for a few months, sex was fantastic! We realise soon though this is all we have, nothing at all in common aside from veganism, and then we part ways as couple. We easily are working together, never any issues or anything awkward between us. Chef Anton recently married Lydia, she is his sous chef!"

Andie asked "Any other boyfriends in your past?" Rada confessed "One or two, oui Andie. In Croatia only I have boyfriends, I am under eighteen so not like relationships really. It was meeting SJ make me accept to myself I too fancy females. You are only my second girlfriend Andie. Never before I feel the attraction alike to you. I fancied SJ, yet with Twin-Flame it is alike totally different, already I could not imagine life without you!" Rada kissed Andie.

Rada asked "Andie, I know Mila and perhaps even Zen Sanders were your lovers, what about besides them?" Andie laughed "Virgin goth! Never kissed. I never dated. Never fricking asked out. I scared everybody off I think!" Rada explained "I know why Andie. You're unreally beautiful! I say this not at all lightly, never before was I in presence of another human close to your desirability or beauty. It's as if all of your pores secrete sexiness! I do feel sure your presence intimidates and mostly scares suitors off. I am honest with you Andie, if I was not so sure we are Twin-Flames, I think I too would be unnerved by your beauty and never dare to ask you for date!"

Changing the subject, Andie asked "Rada, tell me what happened after you qualified as a French teacher?"

Emotionally intelligent Rada immediately got she'd made Andie feel uncomfortable, going along with the subject change "I qualified and soon after I get a job. By now I am officially a British Citizen, which obviously makes this far easier" Andie enquired "SJ and you set out to work at the same school?" Rada replied "This was not our plan Ands, we apply for jobs and it so happens we got interviews at the same school and they employ both of us! We do not hide our relationship from staff or students, although we eat together at the lunch break, we never ever kiss or even hold hands within the school"

Rada continued "Before I actually apply for jobs though, I needed to experience France for myself! Wait one second and I show you. Babes, I have Saint-Émilion

Claret sent from where I stayed, it arrive for me every three months. I go back to this place each year since first visit; I stay in a pretty holiday cottage right next to the châteaux" Rada finished what she was saying from the tiny larder off from her kitchen, returning with a bottle in her hand "Andie, this is their wine, you will adore, I feel sure!"

Andie stated "I know this wine; I've got my own supply"

Puzzled, Rada asked "How Andie?"

"The owners of the château pictured on the label are my grandparents and I was born there!" She answered.

Rada Kostović stared at Andie for a full minute "I stay at vineyard owned by your grandparents? I drink the wine made by them? Little baby Andie was born twenty-five metres from where I lay my head in the holiday cottage? Your grandparents are the most adorable Jean-Luc and Marianne Dupont? Oh my gosh! Aphrodite, she works her magic in my life once more!!!"

"A highly pregnant woman insists she visit her parents, her husband of course takes her, while there her waters break and it's two hours at least to the nearest hospital. Her mother acts as midwife, and the woman gives birth to her first of two daughters. Mum confesses later, she hoped it would play out this; she and her three sisters also having been born in the chateau, she dreamed to do the same. My first five years I lived in France and start school there. Dad teaches me English, but naturally French is my first language. My parents decide to move to dad's native Chester to open their restaurant, Valentine's. My mum is pregnant when they move and she gives birth to my sister Teri shortly after we arrived in Chester. Like you Rada, I found it possible to sound native English copying other's speech patterns. I choose to replicate this actress called Emma Thompson, from my favourite audio book series. I practised copying her every evening without fail. I listened, stopping my audiobook and repeating back what she said. 'Emma' gradually becomes my learned behaviour way of speaking. By the time I reached high school my French accent was all gone. I am unequivocally accepted as 'Posh English' from thereon" Rada and Andie laughed in their mutual understanding.

Rada asked "Do you think in English Ands?" She replied "Yeah, you?" Rada replied "Yes Ands! Weird is it not, we are two aliens, and we find each other!" Andie smiled and hugged her girlfriend.

Rada requested "Please may we be travelling to visit Jean-Luc and Marianne as soon as possible Andie? Introduce me as your girlfriend, I know them, they will be delighted! They treat me more alike I am their granddaughter with every year I visit; being family proper to them is too cool. I adore your grandparents Andie!"

Andie smiled "It's a date Rada! I need to come-out to my parents and Teri first. I'm honestly sure they won't care a jot. I actually can't wait for them to meet you Rada and see for themselves what a lovely person you are! They never knew about Mila or that Zen and I were possibly lovers. Above anything they'll be relieved I'm actually in a real relationship and no longer on the shelf! Hundred per cent sure this is what they secretly think about their seemingly eternally single eldest daughter and big sister!"

Rada giggled at what Andie said and declared "I sent text message to Nika. My family are all fully aware I am open about the gender of lovers. I need to see if my twin senses how I am loving you Andie"

As soon as Rada pressed send, a text message arrived for her "Oh my gosh Andie! It is from my Nika asking who? She texted me as I texted her! I tell her we talk later when I explain all!"

2

Andie stayed at Rada's on Tuesday night as well "I need to go into Kostović today babes, Wednesday is ordering day for the weekend and I am quite sure Chef Anton has his usual shopping list of produce he wants me to get in for him. You need to edit our videos, yes?" Rada stated and asked, as the sun's rays woke them up shortly after sunrise at 5.30am.

Andie replied "Oui, I need to go home Rada; I've run out of changes of underwear! Is it possible I may return to Kostović later, after I've dealt with anything requiring my attention back home? I'll just as easily be able to edit our videos in Kostović, especially if The Coach and Horses isn't in use" Rada's gift from the goddess smile confirmed she too thought this was a great plan. She said "Claudia, she covers a shift this afternoon and needs her parking place Ands" Andie smiled "No worries Rada, I'll see you later babes!" Andie left via the fire escape before seven o'clock.

Andie placed her equipment cases in Scorpy, she set off for Chester. Andie was planning to spend the morning sorting through emails and doing some clothes washing. Pop into Valentine's for lunch and share with her family all about Rada. Heading back into Liverpool on the mid-afternoon train"

*****

The first thing Andie did in the familiar surroundings of her home was call her Teri to ask if she was busy, finding she wasn't, Andie invited her over for breakfast.

Despite the five years between them, the two sisters were extremely close and best friends, as well as siblings. Teri frequently stayed at Andie's during her school holidays over the couple of years since she'd bought her home.

Teri Valentine arrived at eight thirty, using her own key, she let herself into her sister's home. Her sibling was in the process of sorting underwear for washing and placing all the stuff from the first wash into her drier. Teri laughed "Behold, the glamorous life of Ghost Babe! I should film this for VNG!" Andie hugged her younger sister "It's a good job it's you who just called me Ghost Babe Teri! It's Valentine's Night Ghosts thank you very much and not fricking VNG!" Teri suggested "Shall I make us breakfast Andie. Full English okay for you?" Andie smiled in her agreement.

"You're working again Andie?" Teri asked, observing the long black dress, definitely not machine dry-able, hanging out dripping on the washing line in Andie's back yard.

Andie "Yeah Teri, I'm working again" The laughing Teri asked "Andie, do I need to beg for you to tell me where you've been and what happened?" Andie replied "Went to Bold Street in Liverpool. Seriously haunted vegan bar and restaurant. Met five ghosts. Banished a shitty spirit. Owner Rada Kostović became my girlfriend"

Teri screamed and yelled "Andie!!!" Followed by "Show me Rada!" Andie handed her laptop over to Teri "Scroll onto the second video Teri, it's the raw footage from our daylight walk-through. We're not 'together' yet" Teri took the laptop off her and found the video "Rada's a hippie?" Andie nodded, Teri continued "Rada's cute. Her voice and accent are cool Andie, can tell she's nice" In the video, the women had arrived outside the cellar door, having their walk-through conversation. This proved to be the game-changer for Teri, she no longer thought of Rada as this nicely cute hippie "Oh!!! Rada's smile Andie! How the flip did she *instantly* transform into *the* hottest woman ever?! Rada's like scorching hot Andie!!! Seriously, when Rada smiled like that even I wanted her and I'm like sooo straight! Trust me Andie, I totally get how you'd fall for Rada, she's fricking mega-hot! You gonna tell mum and dad about her?"

Andie said "Breakfast?" Teri laughed and made herself busy with her prep in the kitchen. "Have I got time for a shower Teri?" Her sister answered "Long as you don't take forever!" Andie requested "I want to take this braid

145

out and wash my hair, this won't be fast Teri! Can't you have a coffee, before you make breakfast?" Teri ordered "Sit down over there!" Pointing outside at Andie's patio chairs in her back yard.

In less than five minutes Teri freed her sister's hair from the braid "You've got precisely thirty minutes Andie! I'm fricking hungry, don't keep me waiting!" Andie giggled as she went upstairs for her shower, returning in twenty-nine minutes with a towel wrapped around her soaking wet hair.

After breakfast, as Teri gently blow-dried her hair, Andie told her more about Rada and her background. Teri found Rada's veganism extremely cool, explaining that despite having just scoffed her Full English, she adored cooking plant-based and could easily be vegan. She suggested to Andie keeping her loved-up status with Rada between only the two of them, at least for now. Teri reasoned it was early in their relationship, and they didn't need the pressure of 'family introductions'. As usual, of course, Andie heeded the wise way beyond her years advice of eighteen-year-old Teri Valentine.

*****

Wearing blue jeans and a lemon crop-top, her glasses and unusually her hair down loose; Andie departed Chester Railway Station, bound for Liverpool Lime Street. She pulled one of her wheely cases, containing a few changes of clothes and her laptop; now with every last bit of the filming from Kostović uploaded ready for her to edit.

"Afternoon Claudia! Is Rada in her office?" She asked the only person she could put a name to out of the bar staff. Claudia asked her "Can I call you Ands?" Andie smiled "Yeah, for sure you can!" Claudia beckoned her to come behind the bar and took her through the kitchen and into the empty staff room. Being careful not to be overheard, Claudia whispered in Andie's ear "Ands, I kind of know what's developing between Rada and you. She's been married to this place for way too long Ands; it's about time she enjoyed some loving! Sammy-Jayne and me; we love her like family and I'm Italian, in my culture family is everything! Please always appreciate her Ands, she's a one-off!" Andie respected Claudia looking out for Rada. Andie asked "Are you okay with getting hugs Claudia?" She grinned, with that agreed, Andie did just that!

Claudia whispered "She's upstairs Ands, she's spent the whole morning waiting for you to return I think" Claudia winked at Andie, as she set off to The Coach and Horses Function Suite.

She walked through the doors to discover Rada sitting at one of the tables with her laptop in front of her. She leapt up when she saw Andie, running across the room to kiss her "I decided I too work up here Ands, this way we are spending more precious time together!"

While Andie breathed in the exquisite fragrance of Rada, she couldn't argue with her logic.

Andie couldn't not know "What's your perfume babes?" Rada seemed puzzled "Andie did you notice perfume in my bedroom or in the bathroom? I only use an odourless deodorant crystal spray, then I am all good to be going. I own no perfume. I don't like the parabens polluting me, they make me sneeze!"

With a jolt Andie realised 'Fragrance of Rada' she'd been constantly reacting to since the moment they met must actually be Rada's pheromones! Wondering if anyone else could smell them and concluding probably not. She said "You always smell divine Rada!" She kissed Andie.

*****

Sitting herself at the adjacent table, and turning on her laptop, Andie was about to discover something urgent requiring her attention. Infinitely complex and urgent!

An intriguing email sat waiting for Andie in her inbox "Our proposed case we require to be off the record, and we cannot allow filming" stated the heading

The email itself elaborated "Dear Miss Valentine, we are aware you have previously worked for corporate clients who don't wish you to record a video for your channel showcasing your investigation or indeed divulge details of exactly what you did for them. Miss Valentine, we too fall into that category, however, in our case we request an even denser veil of secrecy remains shrouded around you and precisely what we propose you do for us. If you agree to our terms; and we must insist your acceptance forms a legally binding contract between ourselves and you, ensuring our mutual bond of silence; soon we shall communicate with you further to provide details about our proposed case"

Andie knew where the email originated from, they made no effort to disguise this fact. She fired back "I accept"

In fifteen minutes Andie found out all "Thank you very much for agreeing to our terms Miss Valentine. There is a multi-storey car park situated above the bus station in our city. Here is a link for you to read more about it on the internet. As you will observe this car park once was, and unfortunately today may also be, the favoured place for unhappy souls to jump off and end their lives. Please investigate level nine of this car park Miss Valentine. There are members of the public reporting experiencing weird things happening. Miss Valentine, we desire you to cleanse level nine for us. The need for our discretion is many relatives of the unfortunate suicides remain alive and living within the city. Should it ever become public knowledge their County Council employ the services of basically a psychic to cleanse the place of the spirits, we would be facing at the very least a credibility problem or even become figures of hate. We don't wish you to travel to the city in your highly distinctive car Miss Valentine or book a hotel in your own well-known name; we trust in your ability to work around this. The car park closes at seven thirty weekdays. You shall be afforded free run of the place all evening after that time Miss Valentine. You will be given a key to afford your entry to said car park whenever you are ready, we request you leave the key in the County Hall mailbox after you are through with your task"

She showed the email to Rada; they followed the link to the online information.

The car park first opened right at the end of the 1960's, straight away attracting the unfortunate attention of this young man wishing to end it all, jumping off the top to his death. Over the next decade other suicides followed and then nothing for several years. The construction of a three-metre-high fence topped with razor wire on level nine stopped the trend, however, in the previous month a teenage girl, undeterred by these defences managed to jump off the infamous location to her death. Andie knew if she thoroughly cleansed the car park, its attraction as a potential suicide spot would largely go with it. She had little choice but to go visit and do as requested.

Rada asked "When do you go and do this Ands?" Andie pondered for a moment "Friday night this week, sooner the better feels the way to go" Rada grabbed her phone from out of her bag "I booked us a hotel in my name for Friday and Saturday Andie. It overlooks that car park"

This case wasn't so unusual for Andie Valentine and far from the first time she'd investigated in a car park. When she can't make any video, obviously her main source of income, the client generally pays for her expenses. Andie waived aside their offer of payment, considering it her moral duty to deal with this matter asap.

3

Andie finished her editing of their video by Wednesday evening, posting it to Valentine's Night Ghosts but delayed until Friday evening, traditionally when new case videos hit her channel. Andie decided, as she edited, to divide it into two parts. Part One covering their cellar solos and going live on her channel that week. Part Two following on the next week and covered all the rest of their Kostović lockdown.

*****

They set off for the city in the north-west of England we mustn't name at 5pm on Friday. Rada patiently dealing with the traffic queues while she drove them up there in Artemis the Beetle. With the summer heatwave melting roads, they were grateful for the air-conditioned comfort they travelled in. Rada was yet to feature on Valentine's Night Ghosts, their first video effectively going live at 9pm Friday, when the car park case was underway. Her anonymity was guaranteed.

They arrived for six thirty in the city we mustn't name, Andie waited in the car as her girlfriend went to check in. Once up in their room Rada text messaged. Andie walked confidently past reception, into the lift and duly entered their room. "When do you investigate Andie?"

Rada asked before she'd even got the chance to put her bag down. Andie replied "Over there for nine. I can't imagine it's going to take me more than an hour max" Rada stared at her expectantly "I investigate with you, yes?"

They hadn't discussed if Rada would get involved with further cases. Andie figured that her girlfriend was busy running Kostović and wouldn't appreciate being asked to travel the length and breadth of the country chasing after ghosts with her!

"Erm, if you're okay with the subject matter Rada, yeah I would be delighted to investigate alongside you again!" Rada's gift from the goddess smile, she slipped out of her dress and kicked off her sandals "The full two and the half hours before we investigate!" She accurately stated.

4

Eight o'clock a key mysteriously appeared in reception; a member of hotel reception staff knocked on their door shortly after this. Our investigators were thankfully fully dressed, enjoying vegan pizza. Andie took the proffered key.

A brown envelope was attached to the key by a length of string. Removing and opening it, Andie discovered a small hand-drawn map showing which door the key fitted and precisely where the letterbox she needed to deposit said key after she was through was located. A further self-seal brown envelope was folded up inside the first one with 'Spare Car Park Key' written large in red marker pen, suggesting the idea was quite likely to place it in there prior to posting at the County Hall.

They stood with their arms around one another's waists at the window of their hotel room, gazing across at the car park. It was a strange kind of construction, with a fully functioning bus station underneath. It's like back in the 60's someone said "Let's design a futuristic car park and it'll still look fab in the year 2000!" It really hadn't and by 2025 nothing much had changed. When viewed from any angle it somehow didn't manage to quite work as a piece of coherent architectural design.

"Let's go to do this Rada!" Holding hands they exited their hotel's front door and strolled less than a hundred metres to the car park. As there was no filming required and baking hot even at 9pm, Andie was dressed 'any-girl' for comfort in a white mini skirt and top, with Rada style hemp sandals, a gift from the woman herself. Rada wore a typical floral summer boho maxi, with identical sandals to Andie.

Following their sketched map, they soon found the door the key fitted. Opening it, the women were greeted with a concrete staircase and the overwhelmingly strong acrid aroma of stale urine!

"Oh my gosh! The lift, it does not work Ands!" Declared Rada "Level nine we must go, we only have an option of stairs that stink of a piddle" Despite the situation Andie giggled, she begged "Rada, please say piddle again!" She stated "Piddle!" They stepped back outside into clean air until they stopped laughing.

Andie postulated "Okay Rada, we could try to run while also holding our breath, or at level one exit these piddly stairs and stroll the rest of the way up the ramps of the car park" Rada came back with "My dress is ankle length. No way I can run in this and for sure not on piddly stairs, unless I wish to trip and fall straight back down to start!" Andie grinned "Plan B it is then Rada"

They exited the door to begin their laborious journey via all the ramps of the car park up on the way to level nine. Halfway to their destination, they stopped for a moment as Andie tied her hair into a high ponytail in an effort to keep cool. She unwittingly looked like a cheerleader who managed to misplace the rest of her posse.

After what had felt like hours, they found themselves up on level nine. In the absence of filming, the only tech they had taken along was the digital voice recorder, to capture any electronic voice phenomenon or EVP's from lingering spirits hanging out on level nine. Rada would have easily described this piece of kit beautifully!

"You two girls up here looking for ghosts?" This question posed by a man clearly a car park attendant, as he exited the same stairway they'd earlier abandoned when opting to take the long way round to avoid the 'piddly stairs'. At getting called a girl Rada bristled, sensing she was about to vent at his disrespect, as she would have taken it; Andie declared "Hello!" She stroked the back of Rada's hand to calm her. The man responded "Hiya love! I heard they'd given me spare keys to someone and guessed what it'd be about. Stayed on after I'd done me rounds and watch me CCTV for who'd turn up"

Rada and Andie glanced at each other, they'd been called 'girls' and Andie 'love'! Subtly Rada shrugged her elegant shoulders. Taking her cue, Andie leniently allowed this to slide by uncommented upon.

The man leant back against the wall next to the door he'd recently exited, obviously intending to share his personal paranormal experiences in the car park.

Offering them each a cigarette, obviously they declined; lighting-up himself the man began telling them he was called, Barry Ireland. They didn't introduce themselves, keeping with their anonymity as the Council wished.

Barry was a small skinny man dressed in a long dayglow yellow jacket; with a few days of stubble on his chin, he wore a faded baseball cap showing allegiance to the local soccer team back to front on his head. He smelled strongly of cigarettes. Rada and Andie not exactly subtly moved to avoid being downwind of him while he smoked. Stinking like a full ashtray for the rest of the evening didn't appeal. Being upwind of Barry Ireland wasn't really enough, they stepped further away but still able to hear him.

In his strong local accent, Barry shared his story "Girls, I've worked in't me car park five years, I've seen shadow figures up here out of't corner of me eye and on me CCTV! Me job means every day at 7pm I'll walk right through t'entire car park to check everything's okay, then I lock place up for't night. I never come up here on me own once it's gone dark. I'm only up here now for

157

because you two girls are here as well! Early on in this job I heard the sound of sobbing like right where we're stood as I did me rounds! I'll admit it scared me stiff and since then I'll never linger up here long. I feel kind of protective of these spirits, you know what I mean girls?" They nodded in understanding.

Barry Ireland paused to light another cigarette; after he continued "You know girls, from time to time some ghost hunters or thrill seekers come onto me car park. I always tell 'em they're trespassing and to leave or I'll get police involved. I don't want 'em bothering poor spirits; they had enough trouble in life without people poking their nose in where it's not wanted now they're dead"

Rada clearly channelled her girlfriend when she declared in perfect enunciated English "Thank you, we appreciate you sharing your fascinating stories with us Barry and especially for taking the trouble to stay behind to do this! Please do go home now love and get some much-earned rest, us two girls are grateful we have met you Barry and it is so lovely the way you care after all the spirits, we have oodles of useful information from you. Goodnight Barry!" Rada's gift from the goddess smile illuminated her face; witnessing Barry Ireland's enchanted reaction to being the recipient of her transcendent smile did made Andie wonder if she too appeared like she would gladly cross an ocean in a teacup if Rada would only choose to bestow her lovely smile upon again her one fine day. Um bel di!

Andie would have thanked the man and then told him to go away right now as they needed the place to themselves! Andie figured it must be managing her bar staff that gave Rada people skills far superior to hers. Barry smiled back at Rada with his nicotine-stained teeth and agreed to her autosuggestion that he would indeed like to go home and rest. He waved to Rada and shouted goodnight to her as he opened the door back to the stairs and it closed behind him. If asked, he couldn't have described anything about Andie. Rada Kostović had dazzled Barry and thoroughly besotted, leaving to go home, he barely noticed the small brunette stood next to his lovely taller blonde girl.

Being practically ignored was a new experience for Andie Valentine! In the deepest recesses of her psyche stirred an idea that perhaps she could try being more gregarious too, especially when meeting possible clients. She was so used to everyone she encountered reacting to her otherworldly beauty and this allowed her to get away with often being rather brusque. She'd just observed her Rada in action and wondered about being introverted, and if she should also perhaps give more of herself in her interactions with those she didn't really know. Not a terribly gothy way to think, yet as we've

159

already established, Andie Valentine never was too much of a conventional thinker.

5

It was back to quietness and clean air; the distant sound of traffic on the road far below drifting up to where they stood the only intrusion. Looking at the city panning out before them, they felt far remote from the outside world. Although anyone else staying on their side of the hotel a hundred metres away, who cared to glance out of their window, would be afforded a grandstand view of Andie and Rada mysteriously all alone on the top of the car park. They took in their surroundings properly for the first time.

Around a hundred bays for parking cars, each marked in blue defining exactly where patrons must park; together with multiple signs explaining the consequences should these rules not be strictly adhered to. It stopped short of suggesting transgressors would be locked indefinitely in the County Hall dungeon, however, they'd be leaving the city we mustn't name, with lighter wallets!

The most noticeable feature on level nine though was the brutalist three-metre-high metal fence topped with a full five lengths of gleaming razor wire, lending the entire place the atmosphere redolent of the recreation yard of a prison.

They discussed how to proceed with their investigation and cleansing. Andie suggested "Rada let's get some kind sense of what spirits we're dealing with here, we'll use the digital recorder and see if we capture some EVPs" Rada replied "I'll do this Andie, please pass me the device and I call out"

Andie smiled and passed her the digital recorder.

Rada turned the device on and held it at arm's length out towards the fence protecting the void beyond the car park wall. In her softly gentle voice she asked "Is there anyone up here wishing to communicate with us?" Glancing at Andie, Rada added "Please talk to us. We mean you no harm. I am called Rada, and this is my girlfriend Andie" She pointed with the little finger of her left hand, Rada left it running for a minute allowing for responses and then turned it off.

They listened back to hear if they'd captured anything. They could hear a voice saying something! Rada played it back again and then they got it, a male voice saying "Tell mum I'm sorry!" They looked at one another, tears welled up in Rada's pale blue eyes.

Between sobs Rada said "Poop babes that EVP! I had not thought through all implications of what we are doing Ands. This makes it all seem very real! We hear voice of person dead not that long and they feel guilty for causing upset to their mum!" Rada cried uninhibitedly.

162

Andie held Rada close until she began to calm down. She loved Rada all the more for her compassionate reaction to finding herself in communication with a once vital living fellow human, existing only as the essence of the person they once were, and yet regretting all the pain they must have caused their family

Rada explained "Babes, it feels too sad listening to a poor soul who in despair jumped straight to his own death and likely from that exact same spot where we were stood. Yet somewhere deep inside me Ands, even as I cry, I know I needed to be knowing more!"

Andie smiled at her "You're a natural born paranormal investigator babes!" Allowing another ten minutes for her to fully recover, they got back to their digital recorder.

This time around Andie was going to be the one holding the digital recorder and asking the questions. At least she thought so! Rada looked her in the eyes and winked while she gently removed it from her hand and turned it back on. Andie fully understood, she would have done exactly the same thing!

 "Hello, this is Rada again! My girlfriend Andie and I for sure appreciate you talking to us" After pausing for one brief moment, she asked "If you are still here, please tell us your name"

Rada pressed play "Oh" Pronounced 'ore' they seemed to hear but as this was said in the flat vowelled local accent, they couldn't be totally sure.

Andie speculated "I wonder if he tried to say a name, like Oliver or Oswald" Rada turned the device back on "Please try to speak a little more clearly. Did you just tell us your name?" Suddenly "I think I am getting it! You are known as O, am I right?" Rada questioned.

"Yes Miss" clear as anything was heard on playback.

Rada enthused "Good to be speaking with you O! We can help you leave this place. Find peace. O, other spirits are here, yes?" Listening back "Yes Miss" was clear, the rest of his message impossible to understand.

Addressing Rada, Andie said "Rada, it's time to do what we came here for. I know this is new to you. Take the sage out of your bag and light it; as I say the words, make sure the air is really full of the sage smoke" Rada nodded in her confirmation, and did as Andie requested.

Before they began, Rada spoke out loud to the young man they'd communicated with "We now help you moving on from here O! Look for light please. Find light and move towards it, move towards this light, be leaving this car park to be free, O you so deserve this! My girlfriend, now she helps you all to be free of this car park!"

Andie Valentine's gentle incantations, when combined with Rada's liberal use of her sage, soon saw the car park thoroughly cleansed of every attached spirit, and in under twenty minutes.

They held hands, the sun was setting, street lights spread out like a million jewels across the city, the panorama laid out before them was beautiful but above all else romantic. Rada suggested "Bed?" Andie smiled "Mmmm"

6

When Rada had booked their hotel, in the city we mustn't name up in north-west England, her reservation covered two nights and there was actually a reason for this. Ever since she heard of the town, she wanted to visit Blackpool! It was located barely a thirty-minute drive from where they stayed.

Due to the pact of secrecy, even in her disguise as 'any-girl' Andie couldn't risk being recognised in the mystery city. Blackpool though was an altogether different matter, plus she'd also never visited the town before.

Wondering how Blackpool compared to their own home tourist cities, after late breakfast at their hotel, they set off mid Saturday morning to satisfy their curiosity.

Nothing could have prepared them for the assault of the senses that is Blackpool in the middle of summer season; what the town might lack in sophistication, it more than makes up for in brashness and sheer volume!

Three hours of sensory overload later, Andie and Rada left Blackpool and spent the rest of Saturday in their hotel.

*****

Andie's new case video hit Valentine's Night Ghosts at nine the previous Friday evening. There had never been anything like approaching the reaction to any video she'd ever posted before. Talk about going viral!

There were thousands of comments within two hours of it going live, continuing growing in numbers to tens of thousands within twenty-four hours.

Mostly commenting upon how gorgeous Andie and Rada were together and thanking their 'Ghost Babe' for at long last sharing some of her personal life on her channel.

Every single post supported them, begging for Andie and Rada to become the new Valentine's Night Ghosts team. Multiple posts praising Rada, and many comments about her beautiful goddess smile.

Overnight Andie gained a million new subscribers…and Rada's life would never be the same.

7

They set off early on Sunday morning bound for Chester. Andie had suggested "Rada, would you like to stay over at my place tonight? I would adore for you to get to know my home, and as you said to me, to feel like it's your home" Rada's gift from the goddess smile said it all. Driving off the hotel car park, Rada wanted to get some few issues out into the open and talk through them with Andie.

Rada looked concerned "Ands, I need to ask. I sense Zen Sanders and you were more than only the colleagues, yes?" Andie knew this was coming at some point "Yeah Rada, we were more than colleagues" Keeping her eyes on the road, Rada asked "Andie, Zen visited you in your home, yes?" She'd also expected this question "Nope Rada, not one time did Zen ever travel up to Chester from London and we never lived together"

Rada declared "Oh my gosh, that is a relief! I did not want to be sleeping in 'your' bed! This was not personal to Zen, of course he has all of my respect, it is yuck with cherries on top for me the thought of walking in *any* other lover's shoes in your home!" Andie smiled "Yeah, I know Rada, the only person I've ever had staying over at my home is my younger sister Teri! Aside from you Rada, Teri is my best friend in the entire world"

Rada asked "Does Teri know about us?" Andie answered "Yeah, she does" Rada stated "I adore to meet your Teri!" Andie replied "I'll invite her over this afternoon, if she's not got anything else planned. Please take my word on this Rada, you'll never forget meeting my Teri for the first time!"

As they travelled along the M56 converging on Chester, Andie asked "Rada, I would love to know the story of how you transitioned from being a French teacher to owning a bar. That is quite a career change for a twenty-four-year-old woman. Not a thing most young women would even consider wanting!"

Rada Kostović replied "Owning a bar all happened by an accident, I never intended to buy a bar!" Intrigued Andie asked "How could you never have intended to purchase a bar Rada, and yet end up owning one?" Rada responded "Overnight, distressingly I became a millionaire!"

IN THE MARKET FOR GHOSTS
To be scared
Or not to be scared
PART FIVE

1

"Erm, pardon Rada?"

She replied "It is a long story Andie"

"If you feel like sharing Rada, we're now at home, let's not go on in yet. My gateway is automatic, there babes. Please be careful with Scorpy. Let's sit here in my yard for now"

Rada smiled sadly "I do want to tell you Ands, this story is part of chick I became. I agree to sit in my car with you until I finish and after we talk, I cannot be waiting to see where you live! Please ask Teri if she's available later, as I get my thoughts together babes"

Establishing Teri would drop by at 4pm, Andie asked her girlfriend "You okay to talk Rada?"

"My late grandfather was a great man Ands, my favourite person in whole world. It is great shame you never will get to meet him, because I feel you would adore him alike way I continue to do. Life in Croatia was not too good for him thirty years ago. There had been a war and aftermath was awful. My grandfather, he seeks some way out. His friend and colleague tells him about the opportunity at a hospital in London, this colleague is the orthopaedic surgeon. My grandfather, just alike my father qualify as later, he is the cardiologist. He phones the hospital in London; explains he is Croatian and seeks a new life. They immediately offer him an interview. Grandfather comes to England and never returns to his home country. The offer him senior role and he adores London alike I am in love with Liverpool!"

Andie asked "Rada, how did your dad happen to qualify in the exact same thing as your grandfather?" At this Rada giggled "Grandfather, he was mum's dad, not my dad's. He was dad's mentor and teacher in Croatia. They would usually eat their lunch together. This day, grandfather's daughter, who is nurse, she comes to join them for lunch. Soon it is only dad and her meeting for lunch, grandfather was wise, he sees they are falling in love and always he'd make excuse to be elsewhere for lunch. My parents marry within a year!"

Taking a moment to compose herself, Rada continued her story "Unexpectedly my lovely, sweet grandfather died, ironically this was from heart attack, when he saved lives of so many others with heart issues!" She started crying, Andie held Rada and cried with her.

The sobbing Rada explained "This change everything for me Andie, I was deeply lost within grief of a depth like I never knew! His wife, my grandmother died when I was baby, I have not the any recollections of her. Grandfather though, he was my most beloved person in world, that is until I meet you Andie!"

Humbled, she replied "I am so sorry Rada. I understand what he meant, no actually, what he *means* to you! Did you visit London often to see him?"

"Oui, you are correct, feelings do not stop because he is dead. He and I, we had this special bond and always we will Ands. For sure Nika and I visit him as often as we are able. Grandfather lived in England for many years; he loved the country and especially England pub culture. He was a vegan man, the reason I too became vegan. When he die, grandfather, he was extremely wealthy. He leaves everything split right down the middle to Nika and me!" Rada stopped crying "Nika, she loved our Grandfather as much as me. She moved into his London apartment and resumes her costume designing career for a film studio in England, no longer for the negligible Balkan film industry. For myself Ands, pft, suddenly there I am, the millionaire chick at twenty-three! I am twenty-four as I accidentally buy a bar" Rada shock her head in disbelief.

Andie said "I didn't realise that Nika lives in London. But really, what possessed you to want a bar? I mean you're a fricking hippie for crying out loud!" Rada giggled.

"This happens three months on from when grandfather died. Naturally, I am back at work and still I love teaching. SJ supports me through grief and helps more than she will ever know! One day I go to Bold Street to buy vegan boots at my favourite store. As I walk up Bold Street, I see this old, distressed bar with for sale sign. I must have walked by a hundred times and never before I notice this building. On a whim I phone the number on sign, asking how much they want for it. The quote me half a million, for the fun I make counteroffer on phone of three hundred thousand. Oh my gosh Andie, they accepted!" Rada giggles "I have never even been inside, yet I bid on this bar and I win!"

Andie stated "That is seriously crazy babes! You went to get vegan boots and on a whim instead you bought a bar? That is so you Rada!" they giggled together.

"In two weeks contract is drawn up, by now I viewed bar and it is terrible, oh my gosh really terrible!" Rada smiled "Yet I see many potentials. I transfer money and the bar is mine. I employ the services of a vegan architect and big team of builders she recommends. I quit teaching job and I devote myself one hundred percent to turning this place into a vegan bar restaurant. Always, our grandfather, he bemoans lack of vegan pubs in England. I want to create a place he would adore! Kostović is my vision from day one and it takes six months before we open our doors to the public! Andie,

175

immediately it fills with customers and I cannot believe it happen all so quickly. Kostović is busy ever since!" Rada paused for one moment "My apartment studio, this too was my plan from beginning. Obviously I need to treat Kostović finished as priority. It takes another few months until I move in. Andie, aside from builders, there are four people I ever allowed up into my apartment; mum and dad, Nika and you!" Andie said "Honestly, my home is my sanctuary like yours! Mum and dad, Teri and our cousin Cerise. Tell me when you firstly became aware of the ghosts in Kostović?"

"As I first set foot in building I know it is most haunted! Valentine's Night Ghosts comes into my mind and I think of you straight away Andie, but I decide to leave things for now and learn all I am able by myself. Our adventures with ghosts Andie, they must wait as I establish proper business and I take on more staff. With the little money left after Kostović, I invested in my favourite shop, further up Bold Street. That same shop I went to choose my vegan boots year before, had I not got distracted buying my bar! Even today I remain their silent partner" Rada paused "I think I share all Ands, please show me your home!"

*****

"Your home, it is très magnifique Andie. I get lost within your library easily for many months and only I emerge to eat! Ooh, you have four poster bed, gothic in black metal too, already this I find très deeply erotic Ands! The view of river from your bedroom window is the inspiration for a painting! I must stay here for at least one week to paint that view!" Andie replied "Sounds perfect to me babes!" Rada continued "Your office Ands, it is very masculine in taste, juxtaposed up against your own utmost femininity, this is hugely sexy! I must view all photos of your famous cases!" She stood for half an hour viewing every photo.

Rada said "I have the request to make Andie. Yet it might seem strange" Andie was used to Rada's abstract mind by then "Babes, I'm all ears!" Rada's gift from the goddess smile "Please do not wear tinted contact lenses in future, your eyes are one of your best features, so alike sapphire gems. I do not feel your lenses are anything approaching that lovely!" Andie declared "I've clear lenses somewhere in my house! If this matters to you Rada, I won't wear tinted lenses again"

*****

Andie declared "I want to make you a meal Rada, I don't know what I've already got that's vegan. Ahh, I have an idea!" Andie took her phone from out her bag. "Teri, you set off yet? Fabulous, please pick up aubergines, a large bag of basmati and anything else you think I'll need for a curry! Love you, bye, see you soon!"

Teri arrived "Rada please meet Teri. Teri this is Rada" Andie did the introductions. "Hiya Rada, you're fricking hot! Oh, did I just say that out loud?" Rada came back with "Oh my gosh! Andie's double and she is ginger; it is my birthday and yet nobody informed me!" Rada and Teri giggled, a smiling Andie tutted and pretend rolled her eyes.

Rada took in Teri Valentine; strikingly attractive, yet in a different way to Andie and smaller at around five-foot, she wore navy capri leggings with a matching sports-bra top, branded trainers and hair in a thousand natural red curls. Lean and toned, the way she carried herself made Teri Valentine seem older than her eighteen years.

They went through their greetings for real. Teri declared "Cool to meet you Rada, I've watched your solo vid. You were incredible and amazing!" Rada replied "Thank you Teri, I adore your most sporty styling! You are Cancerian?" Teri giggled "I don't usually go around dressed like this Rada! I came here directly from the gym; my boyfriend Teddy works there as a personal trainer; I help teach yoga. How did you guess I'm a moon child?" Rada stated "I too am one, I see many similarities. Teri, you are somehow quite alike yet also unalike Andie, and every bit as beautiful! I get sense of how Andie might be if ginger and eighteen"

Teri was about to open her mouth to say something but caught the look her sister was giving her and said instead "Rada you're kind of tall, oh crap maybe you just look tall cos I'm so titchy!" Rada and Teri laughed; Andie breathed an inner sigh of relief. Permanent intimate glabrousness meant that Rada accepted her as a brunette. Andie could hear her saying 'Andie, please stop using harsh chemicals and parabens on your hair, I would love if will you go natural!' Knowing she couldn't refuse Rada if it made her happy, Andie kept this one secret from her, at least for now!

Teri continued "Rada, your laugh is fricking sexy! Uh oh, I believe I just spoke my thoughts out loud again! You planning on making a curry Andie? Oh crap, please don't! Let me cook!!! Andie's a brilliant film maker Rada but I guess can't be perfect at everything!" Andie hugged her "My kitchen's all yours Teri, thanks. Rada's a vegan" Teri laughed "I know she is! I enjoy plant-based cooking. I'll eat vegan for health more often than I don't Rada. Get out of, erm, your own kitchen Andie and leave me alone to get on with the curry! Why don't you stay here talking to me though Rada? I could listen to your sexy voice all day, ooh and especially all night!" Teri winked at her.

Rada thought Teri was hilarious and saw her as this more hyper version of herself in many ways. She giggled at Teri asking Andie to leave but for her stay in the kitchen.

2

"Do you want a job in my kitchen Teri?" Rada finished her second plate of aubergine curry and made this offer. Teri replied "I'm supposed to be off to catering college in some like five weeks. I'd prefer to learn hands on in a real kitchen, but not with mum! Is this a serious offer Rada?" Teri got treated to her very own gift of the goddess smile, which momentarily stunned her into an uncharacteristic silence. Rada replied "Oui Teri, I am most serious! This meal you make is restaurant quality. Apprentice to Chef Anton, this is my offer. Earning as you are learning Teri. What do you think?" Teri held out her hand and Rada shook it "Rada, you've found your new apprentice; I'm in and also it's a yes from me!" Teri added "What you see is what get with me Rada. I'm a bit concerned I'll be too full-on for your lovely calm vegan kitchen!" Rada laughed "Oh my gosh Teri, you have yet to meet Chef's Anton and Lydia! Take my word babes, you fit into their kitchen as an especially gorgeous ginger glove! You can start on the first of September"

Already fully aware of the answer to this question, Teri joked "You haven't got a sister exactly like you have you Rada?" Andie played a comedic foil to her sister, replying "Rada has an identical twin called Nika, she's already got a boyfriend Teri!" She acted pretend shocked at this news "A twin called Nika? Really? I've got my

Teddy and I love him, but he'd never fricking see me again if I stood any chance with Rada's twin sister! Crap ways am I going to be sleeping tonight now I know about Nika!" Teri winked knowingly. Andie and Rada practically fell off their chairs from laughing!

*****

They were all sat out in Andie's yard, chilling in the early evening sun, her laptop pinged and Andie picked it up intending to take it inside into her office to read "Andie, where are you off too? Can't you open your email where you're sat? I mean, this isn't your library or chilling area or whatever you're calling it today! I don't want you to go. I'm sure Rada also doesn't want you to go. Just for fun, why not try reading your email where it actually arrived? Please Andie! I love you Andie! Thanking you in advance Andie!" The woman in question laughed as she sat herself back down.

"Okay Teri, seeing as you asked so nicely! I'll read it out as I'm reading it 'Dear Miss Valentine, I have a problem I think you can help me with. I manage the indoor market in your own home city and we've got a poltergeist I think! Please may your lovely girlfriend and you come here asap to deal with it? Of course, feel free to film a video! Ghostly yours Phil Gibbons' Direct and to the point, I like our Mr Gibbons! Rada, how about

182

investigating Chester Market with me on one evening rather soon?"

"Oh my gosh Ands! Try keeping me away!" Rada replied. Another voice piped up "I've never been out with you on a single VNG investigation Andie, you've always told me I'm way too young. I'm eighteen and a working woman now, right Rada?" Rada nodded her head agreeing "Pleeeease Andie! I really really really want to go with Rada and you to investigate the fricking creepy market when it's closed and like even creepier! I'll buy a black wig and borrow a dress off you. We'll be like these two crazy gothic sisters out on day release with our gorgeous hippie carer! I mean, who the heck wouldn't want to watch that?!" Andie sat I there n silent contemplation for a full minute. The other two women gazed at her expectantly "Okay Teri, if Mr Gibbons agrees we may do this before you start your new job" Rada high-fived Teri.

Teri delightedly grabbed Andie and Rada in a group hug. As she let them go, she raised her glass of carrot juice and toasted " To two gothic bitches and one sexy hippie!"

An hour later Andie declared "Time for you to go home now Teri; Rada and I want to go to bed" Teri complained "But it's still only like nine!" Two women stared levelly at her "Ahh, right! You know what ladies?

183

I suddenly feel so tired, I think I'll head home right now straight to my lonely single bed and dream about Nika! Love you Andie! Love you Rada!" Teri Valentine left, leaving laughter and fun behind in the air.

"Oh my gosh Ands, I am so in love with your Teri!" Andie smiled "I know babes, everyone she ever meets loves her, Teri hasn't got any clue how amazing she is!" Rada stated "Teri Valentine should be available on prescription just to remind everyone how incredible life is!" They kissed and arms around one another, went inside to bed.

*****

The following morning Rada finally met Andie and Teri's parents. Rada talked shop in French with them, as fellow restaurant owners. She invited them over to Kostović for a vegan meal with only her on their first lunch service off from Valentine's. This happened a week later. They fell in love with Rada like their daughters had in different ways. Proudly referring to her in conversation outside of family as 'our lovely daughter in law Rada!'

3

Rada pulled into the yard of Andie's home in Chester at 7pm on Monday 25th August, her girlfriend had already given her an electronic remote key of her own for the gate. Teri sprinted out to greet Rada as she got out of Artemis and walked into the house link-armed with her.

Andie briefed her team "Mr Gibbons kindly agreed to let us in on Bank Holiday Monday, then you Teri can be part of the investigation without it clashing with your big day at Kostović. Ladies, we must disregard all our lovely Mr Gibbons has already said and investigate from scratch for ourselves! I'll text Mr Gibbons to tell him we're on our way, let's go and investigate!" Late August in England the evenings are usually warm, ominously that evening was chilly, maybe the ghost knew they were on their way!

Despite joking about going gothic, Teri hadn't. Dressed in a pink summer dress, teamed up with a blue denim jacket and trainers. Her minimal make-up easily differentiated her from her sister; resplendent in the same dress she'd worn to investigate Kostović because Rada liked her in it, military boots, gothic war paint and a thick braid hanging down to the small of her back. Unusually, Rada opted for a black maxi dress instead of her seeming endless supply of floral ones. An ethnic cardigan, rose-tinted sunglasses and her hair back in its familiar two plaits.

The three women discovered what it must be like to be pop stars walking the fifteen minutes to Chester Market! Hundreds of blatant smartphone photos were captured of them as they strolled through Chester. Gratefully arriving at their destination. Mr Gibbons stood waiting for them. After brief introductions, he gave them a spare key to lock up after themselves and went home.

*****

Before they began filming Rada stated "I call on Goddess Aphrodite to protect Teri and Andie Valentine and myself during tonight's investigations" Rada group hugged with the sisters. Teri considered Rada a beautiful kook, and she adored her all the more for this. She felt sisterhood to Rada; they were so much more alike in personality than her and Andie.

Andie spoke into her static camera set up on a tripod just inside the entrance to the market "Hello and welcome to Valentine's Night Ghosts, if you're new here, I'm Andie Valentine. Claims of poltergeist activity has brought the team and me along to investigate Chester Indoor Market!" Andie panned her hand-held camera around the market "What team I sense you're asking? Allow me to introduce my co-investigators!"

186

Andie declared "You wanted her and she's back! My first co-investigator you'll know if you're a regular viewer. A woman as fearless as she is gorgeous, Rada Kostović!" She dramatically panned her hand-held onto Rada.

Andie conducted a brief interview "Rada, thank you for agreeing to get involved in another investigation, I know there's going to be many of my viewers delighted to see you back on Valentine's Night Ghosts!" Rada's gift from the goddess smile "Ands, I could not refuse all the lovely people who ask me to return! Thank you from the bottom of my heart for your way cool comments and also thank you all those who visit from afar Kostović since our films. I adore once more I am investigating with you babes!"

Andie paused a brief moment "My girlfriend Rada is not my only co-investigator on tonight's case!" Andie panned her camera onto Teri.

"Does my other co-investigator maybe seem familiar? I'll explain why. I am thrilled to welcome my younger sister Teri Valentine to Valentine's Night Ghosts!"

Andie did another brief interview "Chester Market marks your first paranormal investigation Teri, are you feeling at all nervous?" Teri laughed "Heck yeah, I'm nervous Andie! This market is fricking creepy in daytime when it's busy, never mind empty at night! I'm a virgin at this stuff; I need to pop my spooky cherry! If I encounter any spirits I only hope I don't scream like you when you see a mouse!" Andie laughed. Teri stated "VNG!" Her sister explained "Teri would like to rebrand Valentine's Night Ghosts as VNG" Teri replied "Merch Andie! Please comment below if you think Andie should offer VNG merchandise and if you would buy it!" Rada and Andie glanced at each other and grinned. Teri was incorrigible!

*****

Rada and Andie held cameras, they hadn't bothered with taking any investigation equipment this time, if or when they encountered anything paranormal, at least one of the two of them would pick-up on its presence.

Andie stated "We'll need to do this systematically ladies, each row of stalls at a time until something feels off to us" Teri came back with "Andie, ninety percent of the fricking stalls in here only sell food, do we really think there's like a haunted pastie behind all of this? How about we ignore the foodie stuff and head straight over to the other stalls?" Rada giggled and added "Teri has the valid point Ands, I too say we are heading for back of market to check out if there's anything there first. We always do your sweeping of other stalls if nothing we may find!" Teri hugged her. Andie conceded "Yeah okay, fair enough ladies, we'll go do that and if we don't find anything we'll come back to seek out that haunted pastie that's really behind all of this!" Andie's sense of humour is never too far from the surface but for her to make silly jokes during investigations was unusual to say the very least! Teri and Rada laughed in surprise.

As they walked the full length of the market Teri noticed Rada filming her from behind "Does my bum look big in this market, trēs belle?" She asked, Rada replied "Lijepa, your bum is looking most extra pert from where I am viewing!" Andie panned her camera across onto them exclaiming "Your two's dodgy banter is like so getting cut out in my edit!" Teri declared "Trēs belle is a great nickname for Rada. I called her very beautiful in French because she is. I mean, don't you agree that Rada is very beautiful Andie?" Rada explained "I nickname the incomparable Teri, lijepa, this is meaning beautiful in Croatian. I mean, do you not agree Teri is beautiful Andie?" The two women collapsed into giggles. Andie rolled her eyes into her own camera and said "Oui! Da!" Resulting in far more hilarity from her co-investigators. She didn't really cut any banter in her edit, dodgy or not.

*****

The market space was huge, furthest away from the safety of the exit stood the scant few stalls not selling food.

Rada spoke into Andie's camera "I believe we follow our psychic instinct ladies and sense if anything feels not too good here!" Teri exclaimed "The fricking stall we're stood in front of like right now feels crap horrible! Or is this just me hating old stuff, of course I mean antiques and not you two!" Andie rolled her eyes to her camera again and Rada groaned, but she agreed "Teri, I sense exactly what you mean. Ooh, I do not enjoy this! Ands are you getting it too?"

Andie put her fingers to her lips, signalling for them to be silent. The sound of footsteps on the concrete floor echoed around the vast empty building. All three of them wore shoes making no noise while they walked, but even if the hadn't, they were all standing still! The footsteps stopped seemingly directly in front of them. Andie reached out in front of herself "It's freezing cold right here!"

Normally unflappable Rada screamed loudly "Aaargh!!! I am touched where only you may go Andie! Ooh poop, that was sooo horrible! Yuck! Yuck! Bleurgh!"

Teri yelled "Crap! Keep away from my bestie you fricking creep!!! Aphrodite please protect my Rada!" She reached out for Rada's hand to gently hold it. Andie hugged her.

Rada asked "Andie, this spirit is attached to some item on this antique stall, this is what I am sensing, yes?"

Andie pulled the dust cover off the stall "Mr Gibbons describes footsteps and women experiencing what you've just gone through babes. Yeah, it's definitely attached to one of the items on this stall Rada!"

Andie and Rada flitted between one another's homes in the three weeks they'd been together, never spending any single night alone. They discussed the paranormal many times. Rada wanted to know in detail precisely what she should do if she ever found herself needing to exorcise a ghost. Rada handed her camera to Teri and requested "Andie, this now became personal, please be allowing me to deal with this spirit!"

Andie made her an offer "I'm okay to step back to let you deal with this spirit Rada, if you feel comfortable and sure? This spirit is not a poltergeist or any type of demon. He's this creepy guy, who's carried right on being a creepy guy as a spirit. Don't act out of anger Rada, if this what you're feeling. I know I did this in your cellar, but honestly it was to protect you and I feel it justified" Rada's pale blue eyes were wide open staring intently into her girlfriend's "Oui Andie and thank you! I am seldom angry and no I act not from anger. I adore to do this after what he did to me and to protect other women from experiencing same!" It was decided then. Andie wouldn't have voluntarily stepped aside if she doubted in Rada's ability.

Andie explained all into Teri's camera "Rada Kostović is about to exorcise the spirit connected to some item on the antiques stall here in front of us. We don't feel compelled to discover precisely which item, none of us want to touch it! It doesn't matter anyway, as Rada does her thing this creepy spirit will be sent away regardless of which item he came here with!" Teri spoke into Andie's camera "This spirit preys on women; Rada and Andie, this banishing is all new to me, how may I help?" Andie answered "Rada will kind of work alone during this Teri, but we can chant 'Om' for extra power to help her send the unwanted spirit away from this building!" Teri nodded in understanding.

Andie filmed Rada, who professionally said "Although in fairness I try, I cannot make direct contact with this spirit, which is relief! I send him far away from here!"

Andie and Teri began chanting in perfect harmony. Rada declared "Leave this place you have no right to occupy! I command you in the name of the Goddess of Battle The Morrigan to leave this building. Feel how powerless you are before Phantom Queen The Morrigan, she of women! Go immediately to never return!" Like always, in her edit Andie didn't show the whole process of the exorcism.

Rada quietly stated "It is done ladies!" Her girlfriend and best friend group hugged her. Andie declared "That was brilliant babes! It must have felt strange evoking a Celtic Goddess rather than your Aphrodite!" Rada's gift from the goddess smile "Oh my gosh! Not that strange in all of honesty Ands. I already know well of The Morrigan. That was like so exhilarating! Teri, you need to learn this stuff and must do it next time its needed. Trust me lijepa, you'll be adoring the feeling of power! Oh my gosh!! What the incredible high!!!" Teri laughed "Trēs belle, I would love to learn, however Andie hasn't invited me on any other investigations to scary places with you two!" They looked expectantly at Andie Valentine.

Andie winked "I'll make sure they fit in around your new job at Kostović"

*****

Coming Soon

This Time It's Personal - Valentine's Night
Ghosts 2

Nobody Asked Me If I Wanted To Be Psychic!

Dean Fraser

A Personal Invite into my Paranormal World

About the author

Dean Fraser is a metaphysical novelist, an holistic poet and perhaps unsurprisingly, a paranormal investigator. His autobiographical book Nobody Asked Me If I Wanted To Be Psychic chronicles some of Dean's mostly haunted adventures with all things ghostly.

He keeps fit by walking, anaerobic workouts and running around haunted locations!.

Dean feels that his live poetry and public speaking events embody the message laying hidden within his name.

He likes turquoise jewellery.

Printed in Dunstable, United Kingdom